smugglers' road

smugglers' road

BY HAL G. EVARTS

CHARLES SCRIBNER'S SONS   NEW YORK

LIST OF SPANISH WORDS

cardón, cactus native to Baja, resembles the saguaro of Arizona.

chirinola, "creeping devil" cactus common to southern Baja.

chubasco, a storm with hurricane-strength winds.

maneadero, apparently unique to Baja. Literally, "one who applies hobbles" or "brakeman." Since most Baja roads are mountainous, this has come to be a term for a driver of a truck.

rebozos, large shawls worn by women in many parts of Mexico.

union libre, the official term for common-law relationship.

vaquero, cowboy.

CHAPTER 1

An unseasonal June storm the night before, accompanied by a six-foot tide, brought Kern Dawson to the cove as soon as school let out. He climbed down the bluff, kicked off his shoes, and trotted across the damp hard-packed sand. Two old ladies, beachcomber regulars, were there already, hunting for arty hunks of driftwood. Otherwise he had the place to himself.

Half Moon Cove faced southwest, its crescent of beach a natural catchall for debris washed up by the long Pacific swells. Kern picked his way through a deposit of ocean litter and began to search along the edge of the tide pools. The driftwood, shells, cork floats, plastic balls, and rusty lobster traps held no interest for him. He knew exactly what he wanted and where to look. Today, he thought hopefully, should turn up a windfall.

Minutes later he made his first find, a piece of frosted glass which the action of the sea and sand had ground into a smooth opaque pebble the size of a large pearl—a fragment of some discarded and broken bottle. He dropped it in his bag and moved on. Pickings were slim, however. By the end of an hour he'd collected a few more whites, half a dozen browns, a couple of blues, but no greens. And greenies were what he needed to finish his mosaic.

Disappointed, he scrambled over the rocks to the next cove, but he had even less luck there. Either the storm hadn't churned deep enough or someone had skimmed off the cream before him. All the same he kept looking, stubbornly determined, until almost six o'clock, when he gave up in disgust and climbed back to Half Moon.

The beachcombers were gone, but the surf had risen on the incoming tide and three surfers squatted on the sand beside their boards. Kern ignored them as he hurried past to collect his shoes. He stopped at the foot of the bluff and peered around. He'd dropped his sneakers right here, he was sure, but they weren't here now.

Then he became aware that the surfers were watching him.

"How's the scavenging?"

Kern shrugged. He knew Dave Lynch from art class, a junior like himself. The other two, tenth-graders, followed Lynch around like puppies on a leash. "You see a pair of shoes anywhere?" Kern asked.

Lynch made a performance of scratching his head. "Shoes?"

"Shoes," Kern said. "A pair of blue tennies. I left 'em by this boulder."

His face deadpan, Lynch looked at his pals. "You guys see a pair of blue tennies?"

One of the kids snickered. "Blue tennies?"

"That's what the man says, blue tennies." Lynch turned back to Kern. "You sure they're blue?"

"Knock it off," Kern said. "Where are they?"

"The man lost his shoes," Lynch said. "You better check the tide. I bet they washed out to sea, that's what I bet."

"Sure. Big joke." He couldn't see Lynch's eyes behind the black shades, but he knew Lynch was laughing at him. Probably he'd buried them in the sand somewhere, the kind of idiot stunt a character like Lynch would pull. "What'd you do with 'em? They're brand-new."

"Something new, something blue. That's tough, sport." Lynch got up with his board. "Come on, let's catch the next set." Followed by his buddies, he paddled out through the soup beyond the line of inshore surf.

Kern stood watching in helpless anger, then began to search in earnest for his shoes. Six dollars they'd cost, plus tax. His mother would be wild, money being as scarce as it was in the Dawson household these days. Finally, after a long hunt, he uncovered them in a pile of wet smelly kelp down the beach. Somebody had pulled out the laces and tied them into a ball of hard tight knots.

It took him another fifteen minutes to unsnarl the mess. Offshore the three surfers sat astride their boards, grinning and hooting at him. Fuming, Kern climbed the path to the street. Lynch's car, an old jalop with a rack bolted on top, was parked at the curb. He kicked a tire and an idea struck him: Most surfers kept a spare ignition key somewhere in their cars.

9

He gazed back at Half Moon. Lynch was out of sight, cut off by the crest of the bluff. Kern raised the hood and looked in the most obvious place, behind the carburetor. A key was taped to the fire wall.

He slid behind the wheel, pushed the starter button, and drove off. At the next corner he turned away from the beach and cruised a few blocks into the center of town, where he left the car in the parking lot of the first supermarket he passed. Replacing the key under the hood, he walked on toward home with just one regret: He wouldn't be able to see Lynch's face when the big clown found his jalop missing.

The duplex was in the low rent, non-view section of Oceanview. In the evening light it looked shabby and run-down, weathered by southern California's sun and coastal fog. Mrs. Dawson had taken a six months' lease when they'd moved from San Diego last January, and they'd be moving again, Kern supposed, as soon as the lease expired or his mother decided to try a new job.

His fifteen-year-old sister Beth was at the table in the dining L doing her homework when he came in. It seemed to Kern that Beth always had her face in a book. "You're late," she told him.

"I got held up," he said. "What's for dinner?"

"Dinner? We ate *hours* ago." She crinkled her nose at him. "Are you in trouble again?"

"Why should I be in trouble?"

"I saw you in Mr. Garth's office this noon."

"Oh, that." Kern grinned. Mr. Garth was his Spanish teacher at Oceanview High, also his counselor. The summons to Mr. Garth had concerned a certain unfortunate test in math. "Don't tell anybody, but he's recommending me for the Honor Society."

Beth sniffed. "That'll be the day."

He ruffled her hair and went to his room. Beth might be a little know-it-all but she wasn't a pest like some kid sisters.

From his closet shelf he lifted down the box of beach glass he'd been accumulating ever since Easter and added the few pieces he'd collected that afternoon. Not nearly enough, Kern realized, and there wouldn't be time to hunt for more. The deadline was only two days off; he needed a new, simpler design.

Washed and combed, he headed for the kitchen. "It's after seven, Kern," his mother greeted him. "Where've you been?"

"Beach," he said. "I'm sorry, Mom."

"The beach? All afternoon?" Grace Dawson was a slim, intense woman with graying hair who worked as a secretary for an insurance company. "Is something wrong?"

"Wrong? Can't a guy be late once without everybody hitting the panic button?"

"You know what I mean," Mrs. Dawson said. "It's the last week of school. Final exams."

"I'll get by," he said. This was dangerous ground— grades. "Going to hit the books hard tonight."

"You'll have to do better than 'get by.' " His mother sighed and shook her head. "But eat your dinner now. I kept it warm in the oven."

He gulped his meal, sitting opposite a silent, studious Beth, then washed the dishes and retreated to his room and shut the door. He knew what his mother really meant: *Why can't you be more like your sister? Why can't you make straight A's like Beth and keep out of trouble?*

His textbooks lay on the desk where he'd dumped them. With a groan he eased into his chair and opened his Spanish. For a while he reviewed vocabulary until his attention wandered to the box of glass. Pushing aside his books, he pinned a sheet of paper to his drawing board and began to sketch.

It went badly at first. He tore off several false starts before he hit on a good clean design, an abstract faintly suggesting the sea. In his mind he pictured the white background with sworls of brown, spatters of blue and green. He worked it over again, erasing, altering lines, and got out his colored pencils. Happy, totally absorbed, he gave a start when a knock sounded at his door.

"Kern," his mother said, "it's late. Hadn't you better go to bed?"

He looked at his watch guiltily. Eleven-thirty and he hadn't cracked his English Lit yet.

"What on earth?" Mrs. Dawson stared at the crumpled paper on the floor. "I thought you were studying."

"I am." He tilted up his drawing board. "Cool, huh?"

She frowned at the sketch. "What's it supposed to be?"

"The design for my glass mosaic. Art class."

"Art? Kern, have you wasted this whole evening, sitting here doodling?"

"Mom, this *is* work. My final term project. I might get an A if it's good."

"And fail everything else?"

12

He swallowed. His mother fretted like this whenever she was nervous or worried, and she worried most of the time lately. He knew the reason: money, of course.

"I'm not trying to run your life, Kern. But you'll be a senior next fall, your last year before college. How can you get anywhere if you don't take your education seriously?"

"I'm serious about art, Mom."

"Your father calls himself an artist. Dressing dummies! And he can't even hold a job." Grace Dawson's voice turned bitter. "What kind of a career is that?"

Kern didn't answer. They had discussed this subject over and over, and it always ended with his mother in tears. He couldn't seem to make her understand how he felt about art.

"You'll have a family of your own someday," she said. "How do you expect to support them? Painting pictures?"

"Artists don't starve in garrets nowadays. They get jobs, good jobs, in advertising, magazines—"

"Like your father? He's months behind on his payments again."

Alimony payments, Kern knew. That was the story of his father's life—too little and too late. Sam Dawson was a window dresser, a top man in the trade, when he worked. But Sam never could stay put. He drifted from store to store, from town to town. Artistic temperament, he called it. "Mom—" Kern patted her shoulder. "You're tired, you've put in a long day. Get some rest now. We'll talk about it tomorrow. Okay?"

"Okay." She rubbed her eyes and smiled wanly.

"Promise me one thing, Kern. There are only four days of school left. Behave yourself. Don't—let anything more happen."

He grinned. "I won't. Honest Injun. G'night."

As he turned off the light and flopped into bed he remembered Dave Lynch's car in the parking lot. Come to think of it, maybe that hadn't been such a great idea. Sort of asking for trouble. But no hodad was going to push *him* around.

Next day at school he didn't see Lynch until seventh-period art, his last class. Lynch sidled up to him and said, "Found your shoes, hey?"

"I found 'em," Kern said. "Thanks a lot." He knew he should drop it there, but he couldn't resist the temptation. "You find your car?"

Lynch reddened. After a long second he turned and walked away.

Kern got his materials from his locker and carried them to his desk. He had already prepared the backing for his mosaic, a 2' x 2' panel of plywood. On this he laid out his pieces of sea glass in readiness to glue fast, following his new design. Once Mr. Zumwalt, the teacher, peered over his shoulder and nodded approvingly.

Kern felt a glow of pride, glad that he hadn't painted some still life or strung up a corny mobile for his project. It had been a lot of work, but he knew this was good, really good, maybe the best he'd ever done.

There was a buzz of friendly conversation in the classroom and continual movement to and fro—kids getting supplies, sharpening pencils, cleaning brushes at the sink.

The sharp piny smell of turpentine hung in the air. It was all good, Kern thought, with summer vacation only three days off, and he worked fast, conscious of the pressure of time. And then he sensed someone at his shoulder. He glanced up. Dave Lynch stood behind him.

"That sure is pretty," Lynch said.

Kern went rigid on his stool. Don't loose your cool, he told himself. Lynch is out to bug you.

"What is that stuff, busted beer bottles?" Lynch reached out a hand and fingered the mosaic.

"Look out, Lynch!"

Lynch leaned his weight against the corner of the desk and suddenly it happened. The frame flipped over and crashed to the floor and particles of glass went flying everywhere. In the hush that followed Kern could hear the thumping of his heart. Then some girl gave a nervous giggle and Lynch, a smirk on his face said, "Ooops! Sorry."

Kern looked down at the cracked frame and got slowly to his feet. "You did it on purpose."

"Not me. That was an accident."

Kern drew a deep breath. "Pick it up," he said.

Lynch backed off a step and laughed. "Make me."

From the corner of his eye Kern saw Mr. Z. barreling down the aisle to break it up. His temper exploded then. He stepped forward, his feet crunching on glass, and walked straight into Lynch's left-hand jab. At the same moment he swung his right. He felt the thud of bone on bone, and Lynch's head snapped back with blood dribbling from his mouth.

All that Kern could remember afterward was a pandemonium of squealing girls and shoving boys, and the teacher's firm grip on his arm. Then he found himself alone in the Bullpen.

The Bullpen was a small dark room across the hall from the office of the boys' vice-principal. It had no windows and only one dim overhead light recessed behind heavy screen. All it needed, he thought dismally, was bars. He sat slumped on a bench, waiting and watching the closed door opposite, wishing it would never open.

I hate this town, he thought; hate this school and hate these kids.

Presently a sullen-looking Lynch emerged from the office and stormed out. Mr. Stover, the boys' v.-p., stepped to the door of the Bullpen and crooked a finger. Kern followed him across the hall, his mouth as dry as cotton.

Mr. Stover was a broad red-faced man who had once played tackle for U.S.C. and still kept in shape by coaching the Oceanview Jayvees. He took his time settling behind his desk and sorting through his papers. Finally he said, "I've heard Lynch's side of the story. Now let's hear yours."

"How—how is he?" Kern stammered.

"Nothing serious, luckily. Cut lip, chipped tooth."

"I didn't mean to hurt him, but he started it."

"He claims you did," Mr. Stover said. "That you stole his car last night."

"That's a lie! I moved it a few blocks."

The vice-principal's eyes were grim. "I hope you can prove that. You're in deep water this time, boy."

CHAPTER 2

Mr. Stover heard him out and jotted down a few notes. "Dawson," he said, "you transferred into this school at the start of the semester. Four and a half months ago. Since then you've been suspended twice for fighting, nabbed for truancy, and put on academic warning. Not much of a record, is it?"

"No, sir."

"Here is what some of your teachers say about your citizenship." Mr. Stover leafed through a batch of blue referral slips. " 'Chip on his shoulder.' 'Non-cooperative attitude.' 'Doesn't pay attention.' "

Kern stared at his shoes, at the blue sneakers that had led from Half Moon Cove to here, as if they had betrayed him.

"When a boy changes to a new school in midyear it's tough to adjust sometimes. I kept hoping that you'd

17

straighten out once you made some friends. I think I've given you every fair chance. But it seems you'd rather play by your own rules. Well, I can play rough, too."

Kern nodded miserably.

"Oceanview kids have their own rating chart for boys who land in trouble," Mr. Stover went on. "First time he's called a messoff. Next step down: joke. Then, whimp. Finally he gets to be a rogue. That's where you stand now, Dawson: rogue. Do you know the next step?"

"No, sir."

"Juvenile Hall." The vice-principal paused to let this sink in. "We can't seem to teach you anything here at school. Maybe the juvenile authorities can."

Kern gulped. He'd expected another suspension, or maybe even expulsion That was bad enough. But Juvie Hall! "You mean I'll be arrested?"

"That's not for me to say. But car theft is a felony."

"I guess I didn't think," Kern said.

"That's one of your problems, self-control. You brought this on yourself. I'm sorry, Dawson." Mr. Stover's hand crept toward the telephone. "Anything else you want to get off your chest?"

Kern could only shake his head. He'd already explained about the shoes and the mosaic. What more was there to say? Admit that he was wrong? Apologize to Lynch and promise to try harder, beg for another chance? Stover wouldn't listen. Once you got a reputation as a rogue, everyone turned against you.

Mr. Stover looked up with a frown as the door opened. Mr. Garth, the Spanish teacher, stuck his head in and said, "What's the verdict?"

"The jury's still out," Mr. Stover said.

"Before you decide," Mr. Garth said, "I'd like a word with you. Ten minutes?"

The vice-principal glanced at his watch. "All right. You're his counselor, Bob. But I warn you, I've run out of patience."

Garth jerked a thumb at Kern. "Back to the Bullpen, Dawson. Wait for me."

Numb with apprehension, Kern stumbled back across the hall. Now what? He'd heard plenty about Juvie Hall. They manhandled tough kids down there; handcuffs, the lockup, solitary, the works. It went on your permanent record—police record. J.D. Juvenile Delinquent. Sometimes they hauled you up before a judge. The really bad ones they shipped off to work camp and put to chopping weeds or piling rocks.

He couldn't keep his eyes off the office door. Garth had always struck him as a pretty decent guy. But what was he cooking up with Stover?

At length the Spanish teacher appeared and crossed over to the Bullpen. Bob Garth was a tall stringy man with a crew cut and thick horn-rim glasses. Students who had him as a faculty adviser called him *El Latigo,* "The Whip." *"Como esta, amigo?"* he said.

"What?" Expecting a lecture, Kern blinked. Then he managed a feeble grin. *"Tengo mucha dificultad, Señor."*

" 'I have many troubles,' " Garth translated and gave him a dry smile. "You sure do. Personally, Dave Lynch was asking for a fat lip, but that didn't give you the right to slug him."

"No, sir. I lost my temper."

"Your fault? Or Lynch's?"

Kern hesitated. He thought of all the sweat he'd put into his mosaic, all the hours hunting glass, but he knew that was only half a reason. "Mostly mine, I guess. I shouldn't have pinched his car, then rubbed it in."

"Well, that's honest."

"Do I have to go to Juvie, Mr. Garth?"

"Good question. You know, Dawson, I'm paid to counsel you kids. Sometimes it's a headache, sometimes it's a challenge. So far you've been a pain. But—"

Kern held his breath.

"—you're no dummy. You have a potential. I hate to see you waste it, that's all." Garth unclipped a ballpoint from his pocket. "Where's your dad these days?"

"My dad? In L.A., looking for a job."

"Where can I reach him by phone?"

The sudden change of subject alarmed Kern. "Do you have to drag him into this? He and my mother are divorced."

"I know. But you're sixteen years old, a minor. In cases like this we need parental consent. Both parents."

Uneasily Kern opened his billfold, found the telephone number of the Los Angeles apartment where his father was staying, and gave it to Garth.

"Good," Garth said. "Now go home. Tell your mother I'll stop by tonight to talk to her. About eight."

"But what—"

"But nothing. Beat it." Garth started for the door, then turned back. "I want you there, too."

Walking home with slow, reluctant steps, Kern mentally reviewed word by word what Garth had told him, seeking some ray of hope. Parental consent? That sounded ominous and final. But why should Garth come to the house? To break the bad news in person? No, Kern decided, that was one job he had to do himself, and he dreaded it. His mother had too many problems already.

To his surprise, however, Mrs. Dawson reacted calmly, almost with resignation. She listened without comment, gave him a sorrowing look, murmured, "Oh, Kern, no!" and disappeared into the kitchen. For once Beth didn't ask any questions. She kept staring at him with wide-eyed reproach, as though he'd robbed a bank, which was worse than tears.

Dinner was another strained, silent meal. Afterward, Kern found he couldn't concentrate on homework. Probably he'd be kicked out of school tomorrow, anyway.

Shortly before eight o'clock his father arrived. Sam Dawson shook hands with his son, gave Beth a hug, and smiled at his ex-wife. He had driven south from Los Angeles as soon as he'd received a phone call from some teacher named Garth. What was it all about, he wanted to know. As a family reunion, Kern thought glumly, this was typical; only trouble brought them all together. He'd barely finished explaining the situation when Mr. Garth rang the doorbell.

After the introductions Mrs. Dawson said, "Beth, dear, why don't you go study in the kitchen while we talk."

"She'll listen at the door, Mom," Kern said. "She might as well stay."

Beth made a face at him and everyone laughed, a little uncomfortably.

"I'll make this brief," Garth began. "I'm here as Kern's adviser. If possible I'd like to help him."

"He's not a bad boy," Mrs. Dawson broke in. "He's just—impulsive."

"To you, yes, Mrs. Dawson. But to the vice-principal he's a disciplinary problem. Mr. Stover is going to report him to Juvenile Authority tomorrow morning unless—"

"Unless what, Mr. Garth?" Sam Dawson said quietly.

"First, let me tell you what that means," Garth said. "Chances are that Kern will be declared a ward of the court. The judge will appoint an officer to serve as a sort of third parent. Kern won't be able to take a job, leave town, drive a car, do anything important without the officer's approval. In other words, strict probation."

Kern squirmed in his chair. That's all I need, he thought: a cop riding herd on me. Like a common criminal.

"But another idea occurred to me, an alternative. It may startle you at first. I discussed it with Mr. Stover and he agreed to give Kern a break on one condition—if he works for me this summer. All summer."

"Work where?"

"Mexico."

His mother gave a little gasp. "Mexico!"

Garth swung around to Kern. "You're in third-year Spanish. You can't conjugate a verb, your accent is atrocious, but you have an ear for the language. This could be an opportunity."

"What about the car Kern took?" Mr. Dawson said.

"Technically it's theft. I convinced Mr. Stover it was a case of bad judgment. Call it a suspended sentence."

"Let me get this straight," Mr. Dawson said. "Kern would be paroled to you, on good behavior?"

"More or less, Mr. Dawson. He won't have time to get in trouble, that I guarantee."

Three years ago, Garth related, he and several Ocean-view doctors had formed themselves into a group called the *Baja Zopilotes,* Baja Buzards. They had established a small clinic, financed out of their own pockets, at La Ribera, an isolated village on the Gulf of California four hundred miles south of the border. Their purpose was to provide medical aid for the local people, most of whom were poor and uneducated and had never seen a doctor.

The *Zopilotes* were all busy men, but they contributed what time they could, a weekend now and then or part of a vacation, to treat the La Riberans. They flew back and forth by private plane. The rest of the time a medical assistant who lived in the village operated the clinic.

"We started in a small way," Garth said, "but the demand has grown so fast that our M.A. is swamped. He needs a helper. That's where you come in, Kern."

"What would I have to do?"

"The dirty work. Everything from sterilizing bottles to mixing cement."

"Does it pay anything?"

"Board and room and ten dollars a month. And I'll be frank. La Ribera is hot, dusty, buggy. No electricity. No TV. No telephone. It's primitive." Garth's eyes were solemn behind his thick lenses as silence spread over the room. "That's the picture, folks. What do you think?"

His brain in a whirl, Kern stared from his father to his mother to his sister. How could he think? It was all so sudden and mixed up. From Juvie Hall to Mexico on one fast pitch. The Whip had really thrown him a curve this time.

Then everybody was asking questions at once. Was

the water safe to drink? Were there rattlesnakes? What about disease? Were there any bandits (Beth)? What were the people like? Did the village have mail service?

Finally Garth laughed and threw up his hands. "Kern's not going to the moon. La Ribera's only three hours' flying time from Oceanview. This job won't be any picnic, but I think he can take it. Otherwise I wouldn't be here."

Another silence fell. Kern sat tongue-tied, conscious of four pairs of eyes focused on him. Moment of truth, he thought, as the bullfighters said. The truth was, he didn't know what he wanted. Somebody always seemed to be pushing at him—his mother, his teachers, the kids at school, and now Garth. *Do this. Do that. Do better.* More than ever he felt like one of those caged mice in biology lab.

"Why don't you talk it over with your dad," Garth suggested, "while I entertain the ladies."

Kern led the way into his room and shut the door. This was Sam Dawson's first visit to the duplex, and he peered about as if he were a stranger. "That's good, Kern," he said, pointing. "Nice brush technique."

Kern looked at the water color on the wall, a beach scene he'd painted one day last spring, pleased that his father had noticed it. But that didn't answer the sixty-four-dollar question.

"You still want to go to art school after you graduate?"

"*If* I graduate," Kern said. "I sure messed things up, didn't I?"

"It could be worse," Mr. Dawson said. "What about this job now?"

24

Kern eyed him uncertainly. Sam Dawson was plump and balding, three inches shorter than his son, a mild, almost apologetic man, Kern had always thought. But it came as a shock to realize suddenly that he didn't know his father very well. "Big deal," he said. "Three months sweating it out in some flea trap."

"Mr. Garth's doing you a favor."

"Would you go?" Kern demanded.

Sam Dawson didn't answer at once. He studied the water color thoughtfully a minute and shook his head. "You don't need my advice, son. If it's going to mean anything, this is the kind of decision you have to make yourself."

Some choice, Kern thought. At least he knew what Juvie would be like. La Ribera sounded strange and somehow frightening. "A challenge," Garth would call it. His father was right, though; he had to make up his own mind. Tonight. Right now. Nobody could cushion it for him, or make things easy.

"Thanks, Dad," he said, and walked back into the living room. "I'll go," he announced to Garth.

Mrs. Dawson received this news with downcast eyes, but Beth gave a squeal of excitement. "You big luckout, Kern! All summer in Mexico. And I've never been to Tijuana."

Very briskly, Garth said, "We take off Saturday, Kern. You'll be a busy boy." He wrote out a list of things Kern would need, then shook hands and said good night.

"Mr. Garth," Sam Dawson spoke up, "I have one more question. Why?"

"Why am I doing this?"

Kern's father nodded. "Why are you going to bat for *our* son? Not that I don't appreciate it, but there must be lots of other boys in your school—"

"Part of my job," Garth said brusquely. Then he grinned. "Besides, where else could I hire help for ten dollars a month?"

Afterward Kern realized that he'd neglected to ask the most important question of all: What if I can't hack it? What if I want to quit and come home? What happens then? But it was too late to back out. He felt he'd be letting the whole family down if he did.

The next three days raced by in a blur of final exams and preparations to leave; smallpox vaccination, booster shots, an entry permit from the Mexican consulate. The details seemed endless. And there was a final interview with Mr. Stover. "Dawson," the vice-principal told him, "thank your lucky stars you have Bob Garth for counselor. He talked me into this. But if I ever see you in my office again I'll throw the book at you. Now get out and good luck."

The last afternoon Kern cleaned out his art locker. Mr. Zumwalt had given him an Incomplete in the course and an Unsatisfactory in citizenship. He couldn't blame Mr. Z. He didn't even blame Dave Lynch. The day he'd gone collecting glass at Half Moon Cove seemed far in the past, as though it had happened to some other boy.

That evening as he packed his suitcase, under the anxious eye of his mother and sister, he slipped in, along with a Spanish dictionary, his paints, sketch pad, and a box of crayons. You're crazy, he told himself; this isn't a vacation trip. Still, they couldn't work him sixteen hours a day, seven days a week, down in Baja. Or could they?

Early next morning, after an almost sleepless night, he said good-by to the family and caught a bus to the airport. Garth met him at the first gate and guided him out onto the runway, where he was introduced to a tall pipe-smoking man. "This is Dr. Howard, our pilot," Garth said. "Kern's going to work at the clinic."

Dr. Howard shook hands and helped them stow their luggage aboard the plane, a sleek Cessna Skyhawk. How much had Garth told him, Kern wondered. Did the doctor know about his record, why he was *really* going to La Ribera? And how would the people treat him when he got there?

Then he noticed a painting on the fuselage and stepped closer. Crudely done, it appeared to be a large brown bird in flight. "Supposed to be a buzzard," Garth explained. "Doc Howard did it. He flies better than he paints."

"What is it?" Kern said. "Some sort of emblem?"

"Doc's an orthopedic surgeon. Bone specialist. Bone picker, he calls himself." Garth smiled. "Not very elegant, is it—Baja Buzzard? But the name stuck."

The doctor completed his instrument check and called to them to board. Kern fastened his seat belt and his stomach began to churn as the engine revved up to a roar. Minutes later they were airborne, and the familiar world of Oceanview vanished in the haze below.

CHAPTER   3

The Cessna flew over San Diego and the international border and touched down at the Tijuana airport, where Mexican officials quickly issued clearance for the flight to La Ribera. Apparently Garth knew them well from previous trips; they drank coffee together and cracked jokes in Spanish too rapid for Kern to follow.

His misgivings increased as they winged down the peninsula. At first the country was pleasant and green, wide valleys dotted with villages and farms. Farther south it grew more arid and they skirted a rugged mountain range whose peaks thrust up like giant teeth. Beyond the mountains the Gulf of California came into view, a sheet of dazzling blue that seemed to stretch to infinity. The land, cut by canyons and deep arroyos, lay bleak and barren under the sun, a wilderness of rock.

The moon itself, Kern thought, couldn't be more desolate.

More than an hour passed before he saw the next

sign of human life, a pale scar of road far below. Garth leaned close to his ear and pointed. *"Camino Contrabandistas."*

Kern's interest perked up. "Smugglers' Road?"

Garth nodded. "In the old days they used to smuggle Chinese into the States that way. Later the wetbacks used it."

Wetbacks, Kern knew, was the name given to Mexican agricultural workers who, some years ago, crossed the U.S. border illegally to help pick crops for higher wages than they could earn at home. "Who uses it now?"

Garth grinned. "No smugglers. The local ranchers. A few gringos who drive south to fish the Gulf."

"Can you drive a car to La Ribera?"

"You can," Garth said. "But it takes five days. And you'd better use a truck or jeep. The *Camino* was designed for burros two hundred years ago."

For a while he tried to follow its twists and loops along the coast, then Garth tapped his shoulder and motioned him to fasten his seat belt again. His hands tensed in his lap as he stared out the window for his first glimpse of the village. The plane nosed down and its racing shadow swept over a cluster of houses nestled in a curve of long white beach. He made out the gray rectangle of landing strip and a rocky headland where two small boats rode at anchor.

Kern's heart sank. There was only the beach, a few clumps of brush, and the wrinkled brown hills rising steeply behind. "Is that it?"

Garth gave him a quizzical look. "Disappointed?"

Kern didn't know what he'd expected, but certainly

29

not this. Perhaps a picturesque village with colorful buildings, a central plaza and a church, palm trees and bright flowers. From the air La Ribera looked ugly and drab, the end of nowhere. Nothingsville. "It looks so"—he groped for a word—"so naked."

"They can't spare water for lawns and gardens," Garth said. "It only rains once or twice a year."

They circled lower, the wheels touched down, the plane bounced once, taxied to the end of the strip, and rolled to a stop. Kern discovered that his legs were shaking when he stood up. The last to step out, he had to shield his eyes against the sudden blinding glare of sunlight. And the heat! It wrapped around him like a thick wool blanket. "Is it always this hot?" he said.

"You'll get used to it," Garth told him. "It's cooler in the shade."

What shade? Kern wanted to ask. So far he hadn't seen any plants but cactus and a few scrawny bushes. Even the waters of the Gulf, no longer blue but a murky brown, looked uninviting. He wiped away some beads of sweat and squinted at the jeep bouncing toward them in a cloud of dust. The driver braked up beside the plane and jumped out with an energy that Kern found amazing.

"Kern, meet Sergeant Kalinski," Garth introduced them. "He's our M.A.—medical assistant. Kern's your new helper, Bull."

Bull Kalinksi measured Kern with pale-blue eyes. He was a short, broad man, about fifty, with grizzled close-cropped hair and a flattened nose. Bare to the waist in khaki shorts, he had the muscles of a weight lifter.

30

"Howdy," he said, shooting out a hand, and Kern winced at the grip.

"Bull's an ex-Marine," Garth said. "He used to be a drill instructor, machine gunner, judo expert. What else, Bull?"

"You name it, I been it." Bull's laughter boomed, then he turned to Dr. Howard. "Got a full schedule for you this weekend, Doc. Some minor surgery, a broken arm, and plenty of the usual."

"Well, that's what we're here for." The doctor finished securing the plane and got his bag from the cabin. "Let's get to work."

They climbed into the jeep and Bull drove back toward the village, passing several small boats drawn up along the beach and nets spread out to dry. The ripe smell of fish hung like a vapor in the air. All the houses were built of adobe bricks, Kern saw, but only a few had been plastered over and painted. The single street, if it could be called that, was deserted except for a barefoot boy leading a goat by a rope. He smiled shyly and waved as they went by.

"That's Ramón," Garth said. "Two years ago he couldn't walk."

"What happened to him?" Kern asked.

"He was born with a clubfoot. Dr. Howard flew him out to Oceanview and operated."

Kern peered back at the boy, who looked about nine or ten, and wondered how it would be to grow up in a place like La Ribera where there was no doctor, no hospital, nor, as far as he could see, a school.

31

The clinic stood at the edge of the village, a low white-walled adobe with a red-cross emblem painted over the door and screens at the windows. More than two dozen people were waiting in front—women with babies, a number of children, and one old man astride a burro. As soon as the jeep stopped the children crowded forward, smiling and calling out *"El medico,"* but the adults hung back, quiet and reserved.

Dr. Howard was already rolling up his sleeves as he got out and entered the clinic, followed by Garth. Bull Kalinski lifted out their bags and said to Kern, "Dump your gear anywhere, Dawson. I'll show you your quarters later. It's gonna be a long afternoon."

"Okay," Kern said, and after a pause, "sir." He wasn't sure how you addressed an ex-Marine sergeant.

"Think you can drive this buggy?"

Kern nodded. In Driver Training at school he'd had to learn on stick shift as well as automatic transmission. "Three speeds forward, isn't it?"

"Right. Doc has a load of supplies in his plane. Bring 'em back." Bull handed him the keys and disappeared into the clinic.

Kern deposited his suitcase in the dirt and squeezed into the driver's seat, reminded of the last time he'd been behind a wheel: Dave Lynch's jalop at Half Moon Cove. Probably Bull knew all about that, too, or soon would. The whole village, for that matter. Word would get around. Already the kids were staring at him, their dark eyes filled with curiosity and speculation.

He drove carefully back through the village and out to the airstrip. It took only a few minutes to transfer a dozen-odd cartons of medical supplies from the plane to the jeep, and by the time he returned the crowd in front of the clinic had grown. They did not form an orderly line, but sat in scattered groups outside the door, chatting and laughing and munching on tortillas, patiently waiting their turn as though prepared to spend the rest of the afternoon. Not all were villagers, Kern knew. Garth had told him that people came from miles back in the mountains on "doctor's day."

Bull poked his head out and called. "There's a storeroom around back, Dawson. Stow the stuff in there."

"Yes, sir," Kern said. "What shall I do then?"

"Eager beaver, huh. You really want a job?"

"What else is there to do in this—this place?"

"We've got our hands full inside. You'd just be underfoot." Bull scratched his jaw. "Tell you what. I started a trash pit out behind. You'll see the hole. That should keep you busy for a while."

Digging wasn't exactly what Kern had in mind, but he drove around back and unloaded the cartons in a dusty cluttered room. A pick and shovel and crowbar stood in one corner. He carried them outside and peered without enthusiasm into a shallow excavation several yards behind the building.

Underfoot! he thought angrily. Bull's crack had stung. So okay, I'm not a doctor or a trained M.A. I can't even talk the language. Garth warned me: Ten bucks a month and all the dirty work. Here's where you start earning your pay, Dawson. Show the man you're good for something.

Peeling off his shirt, he attacked the earth furiously.

The top layer was sandy and easy to move, but a foot below the surface he struck hardpan, and shortly this gave way to rocks. He dug nonstop for half an hour then paused for a breather, dripping sweat. For all that effort the hole seemed hardly larger than when he'd begun.

He hadn't noticed any water faucets, but there was a canteen in the back of the jeep, and he had a long drink. It tasted flat and metallic and sloshed uncomfortably in his stomach. What he needed was food. He hadn't eaten a bite since breakfast at five o'clock that morning. But he wasn't about to barge into the clinic and ask for lunch.

Slowly the hole deepened. Kern pried up boulders, muscled them over the side and into a pile. As the afternoon wore on the heat seemed to increase. He stopped often to rest, stretched out flat on the ground with his eyes closed against the sun dazzle. The water in the canteen didn't quench his thrist, but he drained off the last drop and stumbled back to the pit.

Nobody came to check on him or tell him to quit. Maybe they want to see if I can take it, he thought. Gotta keep digging, real gung ho. His head ached and he felt feverish and dizzy, but he picked up the crowbar again and spit on his hands. Suddenly the rocks melted before his eyes, his knees buckled, and he was falling, falling . . .

Some while later Kern struggled out of a black void to become aware of voices and people bending over him. Someone felt his pulse and lifted one eyelid. Dr. Howard's face swam into focus. "Heat prostration," the doctor said. "Help me get him inside."

"—crazy kid." That was Bull Kalinski. "Working in that sun all afternoon without a hat."

The voices trailed off into a background murmur of Spanish. Two men lifted him to his feet, half dragged and half carried him into a darkened room, and laid him on a bed. Someone placed a cool damp cloth across his forehead and forced a spoonful of bitter-tasting liquid down his throat. Then he blacked out again.

When he awoke, early-morning light was streaming through a window. For a minute he couldn't remember where he was, how he happened to be in a strange little room with bare adobe walls. He blinked and sat up and clutched at his blanket. The only furniture besides the bed, which turned out to be a canvas camp cot, was a packing crate on which stood a washbasin and a kerosene lamp. He recognized his clothes hanging on a nail and his suitcase on the floor, and then everything came back to him.

It hadn't been a dream after all. This was real: The clinic at La Ribera.

At that moment Garth eased his long thin shape through the doorway. "Awake at last, I see," he said in a cheerful voice. "How do you feel?"

"Kind of spooky," Kern said. "I thought I was home."

"You got a touch of sunstroke. Nothing serious." Garth held out a battered straw hat fringed with long ragged fibers like an old bird's nest. "Try this on for size."

Kern pulled the hat on his head. It felt greasy and fit too tight, but he didn't want to sound complaining. "Thanks," he said. "I'm sorry I caused a fuss yesterday."

"No strain. Tell the truth, we were so busy helping Doc Howard with his patients I completely forgot you till Bull went out to look for the jeep." Garth smiled. "That's quite a hole you dug. But from now on keep your head covered. This time of year even the natives do."

"I'll remember."

"Better keep your shirt on, too, till you toughen up. This sun can burn you to a crisp."

Kern looked down at the bright-pink skin of his chest and stomach. In a day or two he'd be peeling like an onion. What was the line from that old song? *Mad dogs and Englishmen go out in the mid-day sun.* And crazy American kids who should know better.

"This is your room," Garth said. "Not the Ritz, but it's clean. Come on, I'll show you around."

Kern pulled on his clothes and followed him down a corridor to the front of the building. There was an office-reception-room and the large main room, the dispensary, equipped with an examination table and medical cabinet, and two recovery rooms with twin beds and cribs. Everything, from the concrete floor to gleaming walls, looked spotless.

"It's like a regular hospital," Kern said with admiration.

"Not really," Garth said. "Oh, we've delivered a baby or two, taken out a ruptured appendix, but the serious cases we send to the hospital in Tijuana or Mexicali."

"How did you happen to start a clinic here?"

"Long story. Tell you some other time."

Several patients had gathered outside the door, and Dr. Howard and Bull bustled in, ready for another busy day. They said good morning, inquired how Kern felt, and the doctor took his temperature. "You'll be okay by tomorrow," he said. "Take it easy today, drink plenty of liquids, stay inside."

"Can't I eat anything, doctor?"

"I take it you're not used to Mexican cooking."

"No, sir."

"Get back to bed now. I'll see that you don't starve."

Kern went back to his room and sacked out again, feeling like an invalid. Goofed again, he thought. I came here to help and knocked myself out the very first day. Flat on my face. Get used to the cooking, the heat, the sun, the water. And how much else?

Presently a plump dark woman came to his door, called, "Señor," and carried in a tray which she set down on the crate. Smiling, she gestured for him to eat.

Tongue-tied with embarrassment, Kern groped for some gracious phrase, and finally mumbled, "Gracias, Señorita."

"Señora," she corrected him and sketched an ascending staircase in the air with her hand. "I am the mother of five."

As though on cue several children appeared at the window, peering at Kern with wide-eyed solemnity. The señora shooed them away and departed, chuckling to herself.

That brief meeting, and the breakfast she had brought, brightened his day momentarily. The tray contained a pot of strong black coffee, oranges, and delicious white rolls. But after he had eaten his somber mood returned. He dug out his Spanish grammar book and tried to study, but the words seemed to bounce around in his head like pingpong balls.

Later he started a letter to his mother, but after a halfhearted attempt gave that up, too. What was there to write? *Having a wonderful time, wish you were here.*

The silence began to get on his nerves. Beyond an occasional drone of voices from the dispensary, there was no sound. On a Sunday back home in Oceanview you would hear the tolling of church bells, the hum of traffic, the blare of a neighbor's radio, planes overhead, the jangle of a telephone. By contrast La Ribera was dead, as if a plague had killed off every inhabitant.

Shortly after midday Garth came in. "Doctor Howard's finished," he told Kern. "We're taking off now."

Kern shook hands and said good-by. Garth had seven weeks of summer school to teach at Oceanview High, beginning tomorrow. "But you'll be back next weekend?"

"As our Mexican friends say, *'Quien sabe?'* Who knows? You and Bull can hold the fort. Any questions before I go?"

"I guess not."

"Any regrets?"

Kern shook his head. He'd made his bargain.

"One word of advice," Garth said. "Kalinski is a tough old leatherneck, but do what he says and you'll get along."

"Yes, sir."

"Well then, Kern *amigo, adios.* I'll see you *mañana.*"

And with that The Whip was gone.

Kern heard the jeep start up, and in a few minutes the roar of the plane engines. He stepped outside and watched the Cessna dwindle into the north and finally disappear over the hills. It seemed like the last tangible link with home. He'd been here only two days, but they felt like months.

CHAPTER 4

"Roll out! Hit the deck!"

Kern turned over on his cot and opened one eye. Bull loomed in the doorway, an awesome figure in fatigues and sun helmet. "Huh? What time is it?"

"Reveille."

Sloshing cold water on his face, Kern dressed quickly and stepped outside. The village stood silhouetted against the Gulf's calm silver surface under the pearly light of dawn. From nearly every chimney a feather of smoke floated skyward, and down by the shore a flock of gulls wheeled over a fishing boat. For an instant his breath caught at the unexpected beauty of the scene. I'd like to sketch that, he thought.

"We start early," Bull said. "Coolest time of the day. Ready for chow?"

"Yes, sir."

"You don't 'sir' me. The name's 'Bull.'" He strode off toward the nearest house and entered the back door.

The woman who had brought Kern the tray the day before turned from the stove and greeted them with a smile. "This is Mama Rosa," Bull said. "We eat our meals here."

"And how is the health of the young *señor* today?" Mama Rosa said.

"Much better, *Señora,* thank you," Kern told her.

"I hope you do not have the appetite of *El Toro.* He eats enough for three, this one."

Bull grinned and patted his belly. "Sure do, Mama. You're the best cook in La Ribera." He sat down at the table and speared a fillet of fish from the platter onto his plate. "Have a hunk. Totuava, I caught it myself."

Surprisingly, Kern found that he was not very hungry. Broiled fish and eggs seasoned with green chili peppers did nothing to spur his appetite. He'd have settled for a bowl of cereal and a glass of cold milk. But the coffee and *tortillas* were good.

Mama Rosa stood watching, arms folded across her bosom, while they ate in silence. Bull, evidently, did not favor small talk at breakfast. Kern's glance strayed to the closed door across the kitchen, from behind which came no whisper of sound. Where, he wondered, was Papa Rosa and the five little ones? But it seemed impolite to ask.

He forced down as much as he could, so as not to hurt the *señora's* feelings, praised her cooking, and followed Bull back to the clinic.

Bull worried at his teeth with a toothpick, then said, "Okay, Dawson. Let's get squared away. I don't know why you're here. None of my business. But Bob Garth says you get a tryout."

Kern hesitated, debating whether to make a clean breast of it. "I was in trouble back home."

"I figured that. Garth brought another kid down here last summer. Turned out to be a gold-bricking bum. I shipped him back the first week."

"I'm here to work," Kern said.

"We'll darn sure find out." Bull disappeared into the office and Kern heard the typewriter rattle for several minutes. When Bull returned he handed Kern a sheet of paper. "Here's the duty roster. Tape it over your bunk."

Kern stared at the list of duties for which he was responsible, and swallowed:

1. *Scrub dispensary every morning.*
2. *Keep water tank filled.*
3. *Sterilize instruments and equipment.*
4. *Service and maintain jeep.*
5. *Wash down all interior walls daily.*
6. *Police area for litter.*
7. *Haul firewood for Mama Rosa.*

The list continued to the bottom of the page.

"Part of our job," Bull went on, "is to set an example. You can eat off any floor in La Ribera. But when it comes to public health these people need help. So we run a spit-'n'-polish outfit."

"Like the Marines? Inspections, and all that jazz?"

"Right. We got a campaign on our hands. Against disease. Infection. Contamination. And this here's the front line."

"What do *you* do?" Kern asked.

"Me? I'm the boss, your boss. Don't forget it." Bull gave his fatigues a hitch and spat out the toothpick. "And don't forget your hat next time."

Yes, sir, sergeant, sir, Kern thought. Old *semper fidelis* in the flesh. Do I salute and click my heels now, or whistle "Halls of Montezuma?"

Back in his quarters, he made his bunk and tidied the room and posted his roster on the wall. The door to Bull's room, which adjoined his, was closed and curtains covered the window. Returning to the dispensary, he got busy on his knees with bucket, brush, and suds. Halfway through the job, when he went to refill the bucket, the water tap gave forth a puny trickle, gurgled once or twice, and went dry.

Bull looked up from his desk with a grin. "You'll find a bunch of jerry cans in the storeroom. The community well's back in the hills a ways."

Kern gathered up ten of the containers, loaded them in the jeep, and drove out of the village. Sandy wheel tracks led some distance along the floor of a ravine to a decrepit-looking windmill and a concrete tank half filled with water. Several women were washing clothes, and two girls smaller than his sister Beth were filling clay jars at a pipe that emptied into the bank.

Open-mouthed, he watched the girls swing the heavy jars to their shoulders and start down the ravine toward La Ribera. "Wait!" he called. "I'll give you a ride." He pointed to the jeep. "That's too far to walk."

Whether or not they understood, they smiled at him and went on. One of the women spoke in a low voice and the others burst into giggles.

Blushing furiously, Kern filled his jerry cans, a laborious process that seemed to take forever. Just as he finished, a small boy arrived leading a goat. The goat was harnessed to an ancient toy wagon for the purpose of hauling water jars. Kern recognized Ramón, the boy who once had been unable to walk because of a clubfoot, and started to offer help. But instead, he said only *"Buenas dias,* Ramón," and received a bob of the head in return."

In all he made four round trips to the well. After each trip he hoisted his cans one by one up a ladder to the roof of the clinic and dumped their contents into a 200-gallon galvanized tank. In his head he worked out the arithmetic. One can held five gallons, five gallons weighed forty pounds, he'd hauled 400 pounds a trip, or a total of 1600 pounds in something like two hours, which averaged out to one and two-thirds gallons per minute.

That beat hauling water by goat, he told himself, or balancing a jug on your shoulder, but it still seemed an awful waste of manpower.

Hot and sweaty and tired, he returned to the dispensary and resumed scrubbing the floor. "Why don't the people get together and pipe their water into the village?" he asked Bull.

"Money," Bull said.

"But they'd save so much time," Kern pointed out.

"Time they got, money they don't. You can't buy half a mile of pipe and a rotary pump for peanuts. Something else they got, too. Maybe you noticed."

"What's that?"

"Pride," Bull said.

At noon they took a break for the midday meal and a

brief siesta, then went back to work. Only one patient came in during the long afternoon, a woman who'd gashed her hand on a knife while gutting fish. With businesslike dispatch Bull cleaned and bandaged the wound, and sent her out the door smiling.

By five-thirty Kern was reeling with fatigue. "When do we knock off?" he finally asked Bull.

"I'm quitting now," Bull told him.

"Me too. A swim would feel good."

Bull fixed him with a cold eye. "Finished your work?"

"Almost. There's just the walls and the outside cleanup. I'll do that first thing tomorrow."

"You wash the walls today, Dawson. And every day."

"You're kidding!" Kern said. "I've been on the job since early this morning."

"That's tough. We don't work union hours here."

Red-faced with anger, he observed Bull leave the clinic a few minutes later with a fishing rod and tackle box. Whistling to himself, Bull hurried down the street toward the beach. Kern kicked his bucket across the room. How do you like *that?* he thought. The big so-and-so goes off fishing. Fishing yet! And leaves me to wash down his cruddy walls.

At ten minutes to seven he put away the last of the cleaning gear and tramped wearily back to his room. On a desk calendar he drew an X through the date. Three days down, eighty-seven more to go, give or take a few. Like a jail sentence, Kern told himself. With Bull Kalinski the jailer.

Grabbing a towel and a pair of trunks, he skirted Mama Rosa's house and cut behind the village toward an

44

isolated strip of beach. All he wanted tonight was to wash off the dirt and the stink of disinfectant. The tide was out, revealing bare mud flats, and down by the dock fishermen still lingered by their nets, discussing the day's catch. In the twilight the waters of the Gulf looked purple.

Kern waded out and plunged in. The water was warm, tepid as bath water, and—sticky. He swam a few strokes, rolled over on his back, and rubbed his face, unbelievingly. A kind of greasy gelatin coated his hair, his skin, his whole body. In disgust he paddled back to shore and toweled off the goo. Off southern California he'd seen "red tide"—masses of microscopic plankton sometimes borne close inshore by warm currents, discoloring the sea. But this—this felt like soup.

In La Ribera even the swimming was terrible.

Behind him a voice said, "It's better beyond the point."

Kern turned and stared at a tall young Mexican, about his own age, who had the blackest eyes and whitest teeth he'd ever seen. "What's better?"

"The water," the boy said. "Not so much red tide there. 'Course, if you like the stuff—"

Kern grinned. "I've never seen it this thick."

"Everything grows bigger in the Gulf. Best fish tank in the world." The boy thrust out his hand. "Tony Vela. You must be the new *honcho* at the clinic."

Kern said he was and introduced himself.

"I help *El Toro* once in a while," Tony Vela said. "Interpreter. That guy murders Spanish. Half these people can't savvy a word he says."

"Where did you learn English?"

"I grew up in L.A.," Tony said. "East L.A. Mex Town, man. That's where they invented smog."

Kern laughed. "What're you doing in La Ribera?"

"Same old story—money. Two years ago my pop died. My mom didn't speak English, couldn't get a job. So she brought us kids here to live with her folks."

For the first time Kern became aware of Tony's clean but threadbare shirt and knee-patched pants, his bare feet. "Don't you want to go back?"

"At first I did. Man, I didn't dig this place. But—" Tony shrugged. "It's here, I'm here. It's home now. How do you like it so far?"

Kern longed to tell him what he really thought, to let off some steam, but Tony might be sensitive. At least he was somebody to talk to. "Not so bad," Kern said. "I haven't had much time to look around."

"Come on, I'll show you the sights."

The two boys walked along the beach toward the dock. As they neared the nets the group of fishermen abruptly cut short their laughter and fell silent. What had they been talking about? Kern wondered. Me, probably. About the dumb *americano* who dove into the red tide.

Tony led the way to a thatch-roof structure that had no walls, only the supporting posts. The floor was divided by stout partitions into rows of pens. Tony pointed. *"Caguamas,"* he said.

Kern peered down at a giant sea tortoise. The tortoise stood on short thick legs, twisting its head to and fro on its leathery neck. At the sound of Tony's voice the creature hastily pulled its head back under its shell and sank to the ground with a hiss. "Wow!" Kern said. "That must be the granddaddy of 'em all."

"A real big one runs two hundred pounds," Tony said. "That used to be the main business here. They're getting scarce now, though."

"Where's this one going? To a zoo?"

Tony laughed. "To a restaurant." Sea-tortoise meat, he explained, was a delicacy in great demand. Fishermen harpooned them through the outer edge of the shell so as to keep them alive until they were shipped north to Mexicali and other border cities. That way, no refrigeration was necessary until the tortoise reached its final destination.

"Some job," Kern said. "Flying a plane load of live turtles."

"They go by truck, not plane."

"By truck?" Kern recalled the tortuous mountain road he'd seen from the air. "Not over Smugglers' Road?"

Tony's smile faded. "Where'd you hear about Smugglers' Road?"

"Bob Garth mentioned it. He said the Chinese used it in the old days."

Tony looked back over his shoulder at the knot of silent fishermen. After a pause he said quietly, "What else did Garth tell you?"

"About the road? That it's rough, that it takes five days to travel, it's two hundred years old. Why? Is that a military secret?"

"I just wondered," Tony said, and changed the subject.

As they left the tortoise pens and strolled on down the beach Tony pointed out various landmarks and gave Kern a short history lesson. The first Spaniards came to Baja, he said, under Cortez, hunting pearls. That was how the Gulf of California got its original name, Sea of Cortez. Later, Jesuit priests came to the peninsula to build missions and convert the Indians to Christianity.

Most of the Indians died out, Tony went on, because they caught the white man's diseases. Eventually the padres gave up and went back to Spain. But they left behind them tales of lost tribes and secret caves, of huge cliff paintings and canyons no white man had seen, of buried mission treasure, hoards of pearls, and golden altar vessels.

Kern listened with interest, but he had the strange feeling that Tony was making what his mother called "social small talk." Tony's mind was elsewhere. On what? Tortoises? The road? Or was he trying to cover up his curiosity about Bob Garth?

They came to the end of the beach and climbed out on the rocky headland Kern had noticed earlier. From a high point he could look and see the village lights. Star shine glimmered on the water and he drew in a lungful of salt air. After sundown, he admitted, La Ribera didn't look quite so grubby.

"On a clear day," Tony said, "you can see the mainland of Mexico from here. It's only sixty miles."

"A guy could almost swim across," Kern said.

"Don't try it, man. Sharks."

Tony held up his hand for silence, and presently Kern heard the distant mutter of an engine. He peered out across the Gulf, but no light was visible. Gradually the sound grew fainter and died away. "Somebody fishing late?" he asked.

"There's a sport-fishing lodge around the point," Tony said. "But I don't think it's them."

Kern yawned. Suddenly his whole body seemed to ache for sleep.

"It could be your buddy *El Toro*," Tony said. "He went out tonight."

"Bull? Does he have a boat?"

"A skiff and an outboard. He's a nut for fishing."

"I don't wish him any bad luck, but I hope he falls in."

Tony chuckled. "He's too tough for sharks. A funny *hombre,* that Bull. Always goes out alone."

"He sure didn't invite me," Kern said.

Tony was still staring across the water, hands cupped around his eyes, as though he could penetrate the night. "Ask him sometime. I'd like to hear what he says."

Later, as he was drifting off to sleep in his room at the clinic, Kern puzzled over Tony's curiosity. First about Garth, then about Bull. Was Tony suspicious of something, or someone? Why shouldn't a man go fishing alone at night? For that matter, what did he know about Tony Vela, except what Tony had chosen to tell him?

He couldn't imagine any secrets in a place like La Ribera. Everybody knew everybody else's business. But Tony had made *him* curious. From now on he resolved to keep his eyes open.

CHAPTER 5

After breakfast next morning he asked Bull, "How was the fishing last night?"

"Lousy," Bull said.

Kern hadn't heard him come in during the night but decided it must have been late, because the ex-Marine was grumpier than usual. "Get any strikes?"

Bull merely grunted, but Kern persisted. "How far out did you go?"

"Never mind that." Bull got down on his knees and rubbed a hand around one corner of the dispensary. When he held up his fingers they were smudged with gray. "When I say clean, Dawson, I mean CLEAN! Use an old toothbrush on those corners. Hop to it!"

For the next few days Kern was too busy to worry about any fishing boat, mysterious or otherwise, nor did he have a chance to speak to Tony Vela again. In addition to his regular work, Bull gave him extra chores that kept him occupied till dark, such as cleaning the storeroom and painting woodwork. By bedtime he could barely drag himself into his room and flop on the cot.

Gradually, however, he began to develop a little know-how. He learned to organize his time and save steps, how to cut down waste motion and energy. Too, his muscles stopped aching and commenced to toughen up. When Friday night finally rolled around he could scarcely believe that a whole week had passed. On his calendar he marked it off in red crayon.

After supper Bull left the clinic with a package wrapped in brown paper under one arm and marched off toward the beach. Thirty minutes later he came back empty-handed. "No fishing tonight?" Kern asked.

"Have to catch up on my beauty sleep," Bull said.

"Will you take me out with you sometime?"

"Think you'll be around that much longer?"

Kern colored. Tomorrow would be Saturday. Saturday might bring Bob Garth and one of the Zopilotes flying south from Oceanview for the weekend. "You giving me the old heave-ho? Like that other kid?"

"That's up to Garth," Bull said. "I make my report and he decides."

It wasn't fair, Kern told himself as he drifted off to sleep. He'd worked his hardest to please Bull. Not that he liked the job, or ever would. But he hated to think that it had beaten him.

Later, he awoke to the sound of an excited voice and a light outside his window. Somebody was speaking Spanish in machine-gun bursts that chopped off Bull's sleepy

51

grumble. Kern caught one word—*maneadero*—a special Baja word for truck driver, and jumped out of bed. The illuminated dial on his watch read 2:30.

"Dawson!" Bull called. "Get dressed. On the double!"

Kern struggled into his clothes and stumbled outside. A man in jeans and cowboy boots whom Bull called Luis stood by a lathered horse. "Truck went off the road," Bull said. "The driver's hurt. Let's move out!"

He piled into the jeep and Kern tumbled in beside him and they shot off with a roar of acceleration. Bull drove with scowling concentration, hunched over the wheel, his knuckles white in the glow of the dash light. The road, narrow and single track, curved north from La Ribera along the shore for a short distance, then turned inland and began a steep twisting climb.

Kern braced his feet against the floorboards as Bull fishtailed through an S-turn and came skidding out on two wheels, then gunned up the next stiff grade. From the crest the headlights revealed a deep arroyo which dropped off to their right. Bull shifted into four-wheel drive and nosed down a rocky chute. "Hang on," he muttered.

When they reached the bottom Kern let out a breath and said, "How much farther?"

"Up there." Bull pointed with his chin. "It happened around midnight."

Smugglers' Road, Kern thought, and recalled the few ancient trucks he'd noticed around La Ribera. "How come he was driving on a road like this after dark?"

"All the truckers do," Bull said. "It's cooler at night. Engine doesn't heat up so fast."

The man who had brought them word, Bull explained, ran a few head of cattle up on the mesa. The rancher had been awakened by a crash, gone out to investigate, found the wrecked truck and the driver lying unconscious beside it. Then he'd saddled a horse and raced into town for help.

The jeep crawled through boulders and sand, then climbed the opposite cliff in a series of hair-raising switchbacks. A mile or so beyond the summit they passed the rancher's darkened adobe and stopped above a second arroyo that slashed off to the left. Tire marks led over the edge into a thicket of crumpled brush. Far down the slope, metal gleamed dully in the starlight. The only sound was the distant lament of a coyote.

Bull studied the terrain a moment and shook his head. "Be a miracle if the poor devil's still alive."

"Lucky the gas tank didn't explode," Kern said.

"Bring the stretcher. And look out for rattlers."

They loaded up—first-aid kit, collapsible stretcher, blanket, canteen, electric torches—and left the road with Bull in the lead, picking a way down the steep rough hillside. The truck had left a trail of broken crates and scattered cargo as it rolled toward the bottom. Kern gasped as his light shone on a pool of bright red; blood, he thought, and then saw it was a sack of red peppers that had burst open.

Dodging clumps of cactus, they slipped and slid to the bed of the arroyo where the battered truck had come to rest on its side. One fender had been ripped off, the windshield was shattered, and black oil stained the sand. The driver lay on his back a few feet beyond, apparently as far as he'd managed to crawl from the cab before he collapsed.

Bull knelt down with the light and felt for his wrist, then put one ear against the man's chest. "Breathing," he said. "It's Ricardo, the turtle man."

Kern peered down into the bloodless face and swallowed hard. "Turtle man?"

"*Caguamas.* Sea tortoises. Nowadays he hauls any freight he can get." Bull tested Ricardo's arms and legs and counted his pulse. The driver moaned and stirred slightly but did not open his eyes. "I hate to move him," Bull said. "Something busted inside, I think. But we have to get him out of here."

From the first-aid kit he took out a hypodermic syringe and gave Ricardo an injection in the arm. Then he and Kern assembled the stretcher, lifted the driver onto it gently, and covered him with a blanket. Bull strapped him down and, gripping the rubberoid handles, they started up the hill with their burden.

Ricardo did not appear to be heavy, but after climbing a few steps Kern felt as though his back would crack like a twig. A loose rock rolled under his shoe and his ankle turned and he dropped to one knee, barely maintaining his hold on the stretcher. Bull set down the front end and peered back at him. "Watch it!" he growled. "You need a breather?"

Kern got up, gritting his teeth against the pain that flared through his knee. Ricardo's inert weight seemed to wrench at his arm sockets. He stared up at the scar of the road, which looked incredibly far above, and said, "What're we waiting for? I'm okay."

It was Bull who slipped next. Without warning he stumbled and fell into some brush, tipping the stretcher on its side, and almost jerked Kern off his feet. Ricardo groaned and Kern eased him to the ground. Bull swore. "For a little guy he weighs a ton."

"Can't we get some help?" Kern said. "What about the rancher?"

"Luis won't be back yet. That's a long ride."

The angry squawk of an owl exploded against the night sky, and down the arroyo a cow went crashing through the underbrush. A shrill whirring sound made Kern stiffen, and then he realized, sheepishly, that it was only the vibration of dry pods in the wind. "Bull," he said, "it'll take hours to get him up this way, with just two of us."

"You got a better idea?" Bull demanded.

"Any rope in the jeep?"

"A coil under the seat, fifty feet. But—"

Kern said, "I'll be back," and scrambled up the hill before Bull could object.

When he finally staggered out onto the road his chest felt on fire. He sprawled in the dirt for a minute to rest, then forced himself to get the rope and go back down. The arroyo still lay in darkness, but the eastern sky was beginning to pale by the time he rejoined Bull in the bottoms.

"You took long enough," Bull grumbled.

Kern peered at the motionless form under the blanket. "How's he doing?"

"He needs a doctor. This better be good."

Kern wet his lips. He knew it would sound silly, perhaps impossible, to a combat-wise old veteran like Bull Kalinski. "Once I saw this painting in an art book about

Indians. How they carried off their wounded after a battle. In a travois. They used horses, of course, but we—"

"Art book? Holy Joe!" Bull shook his head. "Well, we can't just sit on our tails."

They shifted Ricardo as far forward on the stretcher as possible, and tied each end of the rope to the front cross-bar, then fashioned a sort of double harness out of the loop. Bull eyed it dubiously, but slipped the rope over his shoulders and pulled it snug. "Slow and easy now," he ordered Kern. "Or we'll shake his guts loose."

Pulling together like a team, leaning into the harness with both hands free to help maintain balance, they started up the slope once more. After a few yards they stopped to make an adjustment: Kern shortened the ropes to elevate Ricardo's head. The travois rested on the two rear handles, which plowed deep twin furrows as they dragged it along.

After the third or fourth stop he lost count. To Kern their climb toward the top seemed like a kind of torture. The rope bit into his chest. Sweat poured into his eyes. His legs trembled uncontrollably. His lungs pumped in and out, sucking for air. Beside him Bull was wheezing like a leaky boiler.

Almost crawling on hands and knees at times, clinging to rocks and brush for purchase, they negotiated the steepest pitch. Kern didn't dare look up. If I do, he thought, if I see how far we have to go, I'll quit. I'll lie down here and die in little pieces.

Then, suddenly, they tottered out on level ground—the road. No pair of ruts had ever looked so beautiful. Bull untied the rope and straightened slowly, massaging the small of his back with both hands. After a moment he knelt by the stretcher.

In the dim morning light Ricardo's skin looked waxy, but a vein pulsed in his throat. Kern let out a sigh of relief. "Water," Bull said. "Where'd you put that canteen?"

"Canteen?" Kern stared down the arroyo in dismay. "I must've lost it. Somewhere, didn't notice, I—"

"Forget it. Let's load him aboard."

The jeep was fitted with leather straps, two in front and two in the rear, so that in an emergency it could be used as a one-man ambulance for short hauls. They lifted the stretcher in and secured it. With Kern squatting in back to keep watch over Ricardo, Bull started the motor and headed for La Ribera, driving as carefully as though his tires were circus balloons.

When they pulled up in front of the clinic, roosters were serenading the dawn and a soft breeze off the Gulf feathered the smoke of a dozen breakfast fires. Wearily Kern and Bull carried Ricardo inside and laid him down on a bed, still unconscious but breathing evenly. Then they looked at each other.

Bull grinned. Thorns had scratched his face and his fatigues were black with grime and sweat. "Boy," he said, "you look like a hunk of beatup marlin bait."

Kern grinned back. Maybe this guy was human after all. "You look pretty sharp yourself, sergeant."

Bull motioned him outside and walked back to the jeep. "Garth may fly in today," Bull said, "but we can't wait. Have to get a message out."

"Message?" Kern said. "How?"

An American named Hendryx, Bull explained, operated a fishing resort for tourists beyond the next point. Hendryx had a generating plant and the only radio transmitter in the area, which he used in his business. "Tell him the situation," Bull said. "Then ask him to contact the state judicial police in Mexicali, and request a mercy flight. *Pronto*. Got that?"

Kern nodded. "I didn't know there was another American here."

"You haven't missed much. And if he squawks," Bull added grimly, "tell him it's a matter of life and death."

"How do I find that place?"

"Follow your nose down the road. I'd go myself but I can't leave Ricardo."

Bull tramped back into the clinic and Kern climbed behind the wheel, wondering why Bull so obviously disliked the only other American in La Ribera.

CHAPTER 6

The road led past the airstrip and over a range of hills, then dropped into a small, sheltered bay, which the point cut off from the village. Five thatch-roof cabins stood in a line just back of the beach like some tiny South Sea village. Set apart was a sixth and larger building with a short-wave antenna on the roof and a front pathway marked with white coquina shells. The sign over the entrance arch read LA SERENIDAD.

This, Kern thought, must be the "lodge" that Tony Vela had mentioned. But Tony hadn't mentioned the American.

A gray Land-Rover was parked in front, and from somewhere in the rear he heard the chug of a gasoline generator. Beyond the cabins he saw a mound of fuel drums and an overturned rowboat and, moored out in the bay, a sleek white cabin cruiser equipped with outrigger gear. At this hour everybody might be asleep or, he realized with consternation, Hendryx could be out fishing.

He found the front door open and stepped into a gaily furnished room which appeared to be the lounge for guests. There was a long dining table, a bar stocked with bottles and glassware, and a rack of postcards. Specimens of mounted fish covered one entire wall. Kern stared about, debating whether to go from cabin to cabin pounding on doors; then he smelled the aroma of coffee.

"Hello!" he called. "Anybody here?"

Without a sound a man appeared in a doorway at the rear. Short and bald and round, slightly popeyed, open-mouthed with surprise, he reminded Kern of one of the fish trophies. "That infernal engine," he said. "It makes such a racket I didn't hear you come in."

"Are you the owner?" Kern said.

"Yes, I'm Hugo Hendryx. And who might you be?"

"Kern Dawson. Bull Kalinski sent me to—"

"Ah, yes, my old friend Bull. I haven't seen much of Bull lately. How is he?"

"He's okay, Mr. Hendryx, but a man—"

"Come in. Kern, you say your name is? I'm just fixing breakfast, Kern. You look like you could use some."

"No, sir, thanks all the same, but I haven't time—"

"Well, join me in a cup of coffee. You can't be in that big a rush."

"Mr. Hendryx," Kern said firmly, before the lodge owner could interrupt again, "a man may be dying."

He had Hendryx' full attention now, and quickly he explained about the accident, described the truck driver's condition, and repeated Bull's request for help. Hendryx listened in silence, stroking his chin, his brow furrowed in a frown, until Kern finished, then sighed and shook his head. "The poor fellow. He's still unconscious, you say?"

"Yes, sir," Kern said. "He's been that way since we found him."

"Sounds like brain damage," Hendryx said. "I don't believe I know the man. Ricardo, you called him?"

"Bull did. The 'turtle man,' he said."

"What a pity." Hendryx sighed again. "That road's a menace. It's a wonder there aren't more accidents. You don't know what caused it, I suppose?"

"No, sir. Mr. Hendryx, please, could you hurry?"

"I'll do my best, but this may take a while. Make yourself at home." Hendryx waved a hand at a couch across the room and turned back through the doorway.

Kern settled against the cushions and closed his eyes, but in his mind he could still see the motionless figure on the stretcher. Within a minute he was on his feet again, pacing up and down, glancing at his watch. Suppose Hendryx couldn't get through on the radio, or that the police refused to come, or had no plane available. Or suppose that Ricardo died before help arrived?

More than half an hour passed before Hendryx returned. "I was afraid of that," he told Kern. "Poor reception this time of year in daylight. Atmospheric conditions. We'll have to wait."

"Wait?" Kern almost groaned aloud. "Till tonight?"

"Not that long, fortunately," Hendryx said. "I was able to raise an operator in San Felipe, up the coast. He'll relay the message to Mexicali."

"It sounds complicated."

"Like the old double-play combination, Tinker to Evers to Chance. But that's how things work here. I'm to call back at eight o'clock." Hendryx appeared with a cup and a coffee pot. "Change your mind about breakfast?"

"No, sir, thanks," Kern said. Eight o'clock meant another half hour. He decided Bull would want him to wait. "I don't seem very hungry this morning."

"It's the heat. Too hot for anything, even fishing."

"Don't you go out during summer?"

"Not unless I have some customers. This is my slack season. Business picks up again after August."

"How about fishing at night?" Kern said. "It's cooler then."

"Cooler, yes, but the fish don't bite as well. Besides, this is a dangerous coast to navigate after dark—shoals, currents, rocks." Hendryx smacked his lips and smiled at Kern across the rim of his coffee cup. "And what brings you to La Ribera, young fellow? Not fish."

"I have a job at the clinic."

"A job? What are you, a medical student?"

"No sir, I'm—well, I—" Kern found himself telling Hugo Hendryx about his work, about hauling water and scrubbing floors and digging the trash pit. It sounded dull and boring, but Hendryx listened with apparent interest, asking questions.

He said, "Just a summer job, eh? Are you going back to school in the fall?"

"I have one more year of high. Then I want to go to art school if I have the money."

"Art school?" Hendryx' bulgy green eyes studied him. "Are you an artist, Kern?"

"Not yet. I mean I haven't sold anything." Kern looked at his watch again, surprised how quickly the time had passed. "It's almost eight o'clock, Mr. Hendryx."

"Keep your fingers crossed," Hendryx said and went back to his radio.

This time he was gone only a few minutes. He came back nodding and smiling, and said, "You can relax now. San Felipe got through to Mexicali. The authorities have been notified."

"How long will it take 'em to get here?"

Hendryx lifted one shoulder. "Who knows? One thing I've learned in Baja: patience. These people don't believe in hurrying. A civilized philosophy." He stuck out his hand. "Good luck to your truck driver. If there's anything I can do—"

Kern thanked him, said good-by, and walked out to the jeep. Hendryx might talk your ear off, he thought, but the man was friendly and eager to help. So why should Bull be sour on him? As he drove away he noticed the Land-Rover was gone. And that seemed odd, because he hadn't seen or heard another soul around La Serenidad.

Bull merely nodded when Kern got back to the clinic and reported that a plane should be on the way, if not immediately—sometime. Ricardo's condition remained unchanged. They couldn't even call in a priest, Kern thought, because La Ribera had no church.

News of the accident had spread, and the small group of hopeful patients who gathered outside were quiet and solemn, their mood in contrast to that of the previous Saturday. Bull treated what cases he could and kept Kern busy digging foundations for a new equipment shed. Emergency or not, the work went on.

They took their noon break, and hour after hour, as the day wore on, he scanned the skies to the north, hoping for the sound of an engine. Three o'clock passed. Four o'clock. Shortly before five a small silver plane skimmed over the hills and circled the village. Kern reached the airstrip before it taxied to a halt. He felt like cheering the young Mexican police doctor who stepped out.

Twenty minutes later Kern and Bull stood beside the jeep when the plane took off with Ricardo, still unconscious and securely strapped on a stretcher, bound for a Mexicali hospital. Ricardo, the doctor had reassured them, had suffered a severe concussion, but there was every chance for his recovery. "It's been a long day," Bull said. "I really sweated that one."

Kern nodded. Now that it was over his tension drained away, leaving him limp and let down. "I guess Bob Garth won't be coming this weekend."

"Nope," Bull said. "Looks like I'm stuck with you for seven more days."

They ate an early supper, and shortly afterward, to Kern's amazement, Bull set out for the beach with his rod and tackle box. He hadn't been gone five minutes when Tony Vela appeared at the clinic door. Jaunty looking in a hula shirt and a tarnished yachtsman cap, Tony grinned and said, "Hiya, man. Much excitement around here today, huh?"

"Hi," Kern said, glad to see him in spite of his weariness. "How've you been?"

"Busy. I work for a living. What's the scoop on the truck driver?"

Kern described the accident scene and told him what the doctor had said. Ricardo was lucky to be alive.

"Some luck," Tony said. "I'd like to see where he went over. How's about driving me up there in the jeep?"

"Tonight? What for?"

Tony faced around toward the Gulf, his eyes squinted

64

almost shut against the sunset glare on the water. From Mama Rosa's house Kern could hear the clatter of dishes, and down the street a dog barked. Then an outboard motor coughed and exploded into life. Moments later a lone figure in a small boat putt-putted out to sea. "There goes your boss," Tony said.

"He'd skin me alive if I took the jeep without permission."

"He won't be back till late," Tony said. "We've got time."

"How do you know? Anyway, what's the point? Haven't you ever seen a wrecked truck?"

"Look—" Tony glanced up and down the road as though to make sure no one could eavesdrop. "I've got a hunch Ricardo is mixed up in some smuggling racket."

"What's there to smuggle around here?" Kern demanded. "Turtles?"

"Dope, maybe. A fast boat could run a load across from the mainland in one night, easy. Then somebody hauls it north to the border, sneaks it over the back way."

"Dope?" Kern tried to recall what he'd read about the international traffic in narcotics. It seemed impossible that a sleepy, isolated village like La Ribera could be involved. And yet, it's very isolation might appeal to smugglers. Others had used it as a way station in the past. "Why Ricardo? He's not the only trucker."

"Funny thing about Ricardo," Tony said. "Every other trucker carries a spare driver, a buddy to spell him at the wheel and help with repairs. Ricardo traveled alone."

Like Bull Kalinski, Kern thought instantly, and felt a twinge of disloyalty. But why did Bull go out alone night after night, when even he admitted the fishing was poor? And why tonight, after a man-killing day, when he must have been bone tired? El Toro wasn't superhuman.

"You got any ideas?" Tony asked.

"Sounds crazy to me. Just because we heard a boat the other night."

"I've heard that boat before, a big twin-screw job, riding dark. Then *z-a-p!* She's gone! You tell me where. And why."

"Hugo Hendryx has a power cruiser," Kern said. "I saw it today."

"Fat old Hugo." Tony laughed. "Can you see him running dope?"

Kern shook his head. But then, he couldn't picture Bull as a smuggler either, not without some proof. All Tony had were a few vague suspicions.

"I'll make you a deal," Tony said. "You take me up the road tonight, I'll take you fishing."

"Fishing in the Gulf? When?"

"Tomorrow's Sunday. How about it? You chicken, man?"

Kern hesitated, torn between caution and curiosity. It wasn't as though Bull had forbidden him to take the jeep. He could drive to the arroyo and back in two hours, long before Bull usually came home. "Who's chicken? You bought yourself a ride."

He got the keys off the office hook and they hopped into the jeep. The road up the coast and into the hills seemed less rugged in daylight, but Kern drove carefully, in low gear most of the way. To cross the first arroyo he shifted into four-wheel-drive and crept up to the mesa. There was no sign of the rancher when they passed the adobe and he felt a tingle of excitement as they neared the rim of the second arroyo. Not that it was likely, but suppose—just suppose—they did find something!

Tony leaped out as soon as he pulled to a stop, stared down at the overturned truck, then began to search on his hands and knees. Others had been there earlier in the day tracking the ground with footprints and trampling the brush. And someone, obviously with tremendous effort, had hauled every piece of scattered freight up to the road and carted it off. The hillside was bare.

"Couple of other truckers salvaged the stuff," Tony explained. "They'll take over Ricardo's run."

"Then we're too late."

"Maybe not. And maybe this wasn't an accident."

"How do you figure that?" Kern said.

"Could be somebody jimmied the steering gear, or the brakes. Hijackers."

Kern grinned. "You've seen too many old gangster movies."

The light was fading fast, so he got a torch from the jeep and in minutes they scrambled down the slope that had taken him and Bull an agonizing hour and a half to climb the night before. The truck looked more derelict than ever, stripped of almost every usable item, like the carcass of some beast plucked by vultures. Even the seat cushion was gone. "They sure picked it clean," Kern said.

"Searched it," Tony said. "Somebody did."

"There's your hijacker." Kern pointed at a large

67

ragged hole in the left front tire, which was worn down to the casing. "Blowout. No wonder Ricardo lost control and went over."

Tony scowled at the tire as if it were a mortal enemy and poked under the hood with the torch. "Last night," he said, "did you leave El Toro alone with the truck any time?"

"No—" But he had left Bull alone for quite a while when he'd climbed to the road to get the rope. And Kern remembered something else. Last night Bull had left the clinic with a package wrapped in brown paper and tied with string. There wasn't a post office in La Ribera, so where had he taken the package? To Ricardo for delivery? "You don't really think Bull's a dope runner?"

"An evil thought, man. I hope I'm wrong. But—" Tony left the sentence unfinished and squeezed into the cab.

It was almost dark, and Kern turned his back to a hot dry wind that suddenly swooped down the arroyo, twisting up dust devils. The sand stung his eyes, so he moved behind the truck body, where he and Bull had first found Ricardo. As the brush danced and swayed, a light-colored object in the next clump caught his glance. He waited for the wind to subside, then walked forward and reached in gingerly, mindful of rattlers.

"Tony!" he yelled. "Over here! Bring the light. Quick!"

CHAPTER 7

Tony came running from the truck and shone his torch on the object that Kern held in his cupped hands. It was a clay vessel or jug of some kind, about ten inches high, with a narrow mouth and neck swelling out to a fat round base. The handle had been shaped into the figure of a monkey, whose outstretched paws rested on the neck and whose lips touched the rim, as though in the act of drinking. "Ugly little devil," Tony said. "What is it?"

"Beats me," Kern said. "I spotted it under this bush."

"Anything in it?"

Kern shook it gently against his ear, squeezed two fingers down the neck and felt around, then turned the jug upside down. Nothing fell out.

"Looks like that tourist junk they sell in T-Town." Tony's voice was flat with disappointment. "You can buy 'em on any corner for a couple of pesos."

T-Town, Kern knew, was Tony's name for Tijuana, the border city. Every day thousands of American visitors poured through the international gate to shop for Mexican souvenirs and curios at bargain prices. He stared at the crude designs scratched deep into the jug's sides and rubbed the smooth worn surface. "It looks old, Tony. It *feels* old."

"Junk," Tony repeated. "They fake that age bit for *turistas*."

"How do you suppose it got here?"

Tony shrugged and turned away, no longer interested.

Kern considered. When the truck overturned, possibly it had hurled the jug out. Chances were, though, the jug would have shattered. The other possibility that occurred to him was so fantastic he didn't mention it to Tony. He didn't believe it himself. But maybe Ricardo had been trying to hide the jug in the brush and blacked out before he could finish the job.

He knelt down and examined the sand for footprints, but too many other searchers already had tracked up the arroyo. He'd been lucky, that was all, or sharper-eyed. Ricardo's secret—if Ricardo had a secret—was locked in his brain in a hospital hundreds of miles away.

"False alarm," Tony said. "You seen enough?"

More than enough, Kern said. This return to the wrecked truck depressed him, and now he began to worry. They had been gone longer than two hours, and he still had some bad mountain road to drive after dark. He hurried Tony up the hillside to the jeep and wrapped the jug in his jacket.

"What you gonna do with that?" Tony said. "Use it for old razor blades?"

"Tony, is there something else a guy could smuggle?"

"Like what?"

"What brought the Spaniards here in the first place—pearls. Or gold maybe. Or that buried mission treasure you were talking about."

"Personally, I never bought that treasure yarn," Tony said. "But I still say something's fishy, and I don't mean barracuda."

Preoccupied with steep grades and hairpin curves, Kern drove back to La Ribera in silence, and Tony, too, was quiet, absorbed in his own thoughts. Their outing had been a waste of time and gasoline. Kern told himself he'd run a risk for nothing. And yet he had the strange illogical feeling that Tony might be halfway right.

Not a light shone at any window, and the village lay still and peaceful in the starlight. The night smelled of salt air and kelp and—as always—of fish. The only sound was the soft hiss of waves on the beach. It seemed familiar and reassuring, but Kern shivered involuntarily.

"That's my pad," Tony said, and pointed out a house beyond the turtle pens. "See you tomorrow."

"I've never been ocean fishing," Kern admitted.

"I'll give you my course in five easy lessons. Money-back guarantee. *Buenas noches.*"

Kern drove up the deserted road and parked behind the clinic. Replacing the keys in the office, he carried the jug to his room and lit his lamp. In the light the carved monkey figure that formed the handle looked grotesque, almost comical, as though at any instant it might lift a paw and thumb its nose at the beholder. He fingered the designs on the base, speculating whether they were merely ornamental or had some meaning, then stiffened at the sound of footsteps and hastily pushed the jug from sight under his cot.

Bull Kalinski appeared in the doorway, clad in pajama bottoms.

"You—you're home early," Kern stammered.

"Where've you been in the jeep?" Bull's voice rasped like a file.

"Up on the mesa. At the wreck."

"You drove clear up there tonight? Why?"

Kern moistened his lips. He couldn't shift the blame on Tony Vela. Nor could he say, *Because I suspect you of something crooked.* And then an excuse occurred to him, a feeble one but safer than the truth. "I was looking for that canteen. The one I lost last night."

"You find it?"

"No, everything had been taken away."

Bull's chest rose and fell, his eyes bleak with skepticism as he studied Kern. "You're lying."

Kern stared back at him, stubbornly silent.

"Have it your way, Dawson. But that jeep's a piece of valuable equipment. We use it to help save lives, not for joy rides. What if you'd smashed it up tonight?"

"I know how to drive," Kern protested.

"You're how old—sixteen? Been driving a year maybe. That makes you an expert?"

"I was careful. Nothing happened."

"Remember that kid I told you about who came here last summer? The seven-day wonder. Later we found out he had a record back home. For heisting cars."

Kern flushed as he thought of the incident of Dave Lynch's jalopy. "I didn't steal your darn jeep! Get off my back, will you!"

72

"Last night you did okay," Bull said. "Too bad you fouled up tonight. So, as of now, you're restricted."

"Restricted?"

"To the village. You don't go any place without my say-so. That's an order, Dawson."

Kern's jaw dropped. "But—but I'm going fishing tomorrow."

"Tomorrow I got a job for you. Maybe you'll learn to shape up."

"Shape up!" Kern was almost shouting. "What is this —boot camp? I'm not a Marine."

"Mister—" Bull fisted one big hand and rubbed his knuckles along his jaw. "I warned you once. Next time you won't get off so easy." He about-faced—even in bare feet he did it with military precision—and went back to his room.

Kern glowered at the empty doorway and slammed his hat down on his cot. Restricted! He can't do that to me! I'll show him—I'll—

You'll do what, Dawson? he asked himself. Simmer down, boy. Use your head. You took a chance and you got caught. Next time be smart. Like it or not, you've got to live with the big ape for at least another week.

Next morning at breakfast, Bull acted as though nothing had happened between them. He joked with Mama Rosa, teased her about her cooking, and winked at Kern. Kern ignored him, eating in mulish silence. Afterward, Bull got an ax and bucksaw from the storeroom and carried them to the jeep.

"Today," he said, "you're hauling firewood. Mama Rosa's running low."

"Aren't you scared I'll take off again?"

Bull gave him a stony look and sketched a map in the dirt. Five miles up the coast, he said, there was a beach where driftwood collected. That was the nearest supply, not counting brush, which gave off too little heat to cook *tortillas* properly. Mama Rosa's stove took two-foot lengths, nothing longer.

"Why doesn't Papa Rosa haul his own wood?" Kern said.

"He's dead, that's why."

"How about those kids? I never see them around."

"They're at summer school in Santa Ynez," Bull said. "You wanta eat, you go cut some wood. Like maybe half a cord."

Kern scratched out a note for Tony: "Can't go fishing today— Sor—eee," taped it to the door, and stomped back to the jeep.

"Watch it when you hit those dunes," Bull told him. "Drift sand."

Yeah, yeah, yeah, Kern thought. Wisdom from the Great White Father. A peachy keen way to spend Sunday.

North of La Ribera, wheel tracks forked off the main road, hugging the coast. They roller-coastered over a series of gullies, twin ruts that grew fainter with every mile. Scabrous black rock, barren of all plant life, tilted up from the sea like seams of coal. Not even the cholla cactus found roothold. Then the first tawny-colored dune loomed ahead. Kern downshifted, floored the gas pedal, and gunned for the top.

The wheels spun, lost momentum, and chewed in deep. He slammed into reverse and tried to rock free, spraying a rooster tail of sand. Cuss words, gas fumes, and the stink of scorched rubber filled the air. Resignedly Kern got out to look. The jeep was bogged down to the axles front and rear.

Five more yards and he'd have made it. Five miserable yards. El Toro's jeep came equipped with two jacks, two shovels, and even chains for snow. But no roll of chicken wire or canvas strips. Which left two choices: He could hike back to La Ribera and ask some trucker for a tow. Or, he could dig out.

Kern's jaw set. In his mind he saw the sly grins of the villagers: *that crazy gringo kid, stuck in the sand.* And Bull! He'd never hear the end of it from Bull.

In the close morning heat he dug steadily for an hour, then tried again. He gained a yard or so and sank in deeper than before. As he surveyed the stalled jeep in helpless frustration, he wondered if Bull had sent him here on purpose, hoping he might get stuck. Maybe Bull wanted him out of the way for some reason.

He climbed to the crest of the dune, where he could see the beach nearby, and once again felt awe at the empty desolation of this country. The wind had erased every wheel track and footprint. Nothing moved across the dunes or the glittering sea to his right. No help in sight, he thought, not even a fisherman's shanty. You're on your own, chum, so play it cool.

Plowing through loose ankle-deep sand, Kern made his way on foot to the beach. Every kind of wood—the flotsam of the Gulf—had washed up on the shore. Quickly he gathered an armload of broken boards and staggered back to the jeep. Alternating the two jacks, he levered it up inch by inch until he could build a platform under each wheel. Then he got the gauge from the tool kit and reduced the air in the iron-hard tires from thirty to ten pounds pressure.

With a prayer and a roar of exhaust he gunned the motor once more. The jeep shuddered and churned, bucking for traction, then burst from its sandy prison and rolled smoothly over the dunes and down to the beach.

Unlike Half Moon Cove back home, this had a wild, lonely look, almost as if it resented human intruders. A pelican eyed him warily from the shallows and took flight. Squinting through the offshore heat haze, he made out a long humpbacked island shaped like a lizard and thought of Hugo Hendryx, the resort owner, who had called these waters dangerous.

Strangely, he felt no urge to beachcomb, to hunt for bits of sand-blasted glass, although surely this was virgin territory. He sawed up a jeepload of wood and retraced his route over the dunes without difficulty on the deflated tires. On reaching the road he stopped and pumped them up by hand, a backbreaking chore under a scorching sun. One short week ago, he thought with a touch of pride, he would have conked out.

At least Bull couldn't crow over him, say, "I told you so."

By the time he returned to the clinic, however, Bull was gone. Kern stacked the wood behind Mama Rosa's house, decided it was too late for a second trip, and went to the dispensary for a pair of tweezers to pick the splinters out of his hands. Minutes later Tony Vela poked his head in.

"Some fisherman you are," Tony said. "Where you been all day?"

Kern told him.

"El Toro grounded you? For taking the jeep?" Tony gave an outraged squawk. "The fink!"

"I had to lie," Kern said. "He knew I was lying. That's what made him so mad."

Tony shook his head in commiseration. "My fault, man. I talked you into that deal last night. Maybe he smelled a rat—me."

"Tony, I've been thinking. About that pot we found." Kern led the way to his room, pulled the clay vessel from under his cot, and unwrapped it.

"You show this to Bull?" Tony said.

"Un-unh. I wish I knew where to hide it."

"Hide it? Whose gonna steal a mud monkey?"

"I have a hunch it's old. Could be worth something." Kern filled a bucket of water at the tap and with a rag carefully began to wash away the dust and dirt that clung to the jug. Gradually it took on a dark reddish sheen, the look of glaze fired at high temperature. "I took a ceramics course once," he said. "The chemical formulas for mixing your clay and glaze can get pretty technical."

"Ceramics?" Tony said. "You an artist?"

"Sure, me and Picasso." Kern filled the jug with water and swirled it around and almost dropped it on the floor as the monkey emitted a thin piping whistle.

"Hey!" Tony's eyes bugged out. "Did you hear that?"

Kern stared at the red monkey face in disbelief, and the skin on the back of his neck prickled. It was almost as if the creature had a mind and will of its own.

"Do it again, Kern."

Kern dried his hands, emptied the jug into the bucket, and slowly refilled it. Once again the monkey gave off a shrill whistle. Three more times he tried and each time the monkey whistled, an eerie high-pitched note that sounded neither animal nor human. Carrying the jug outside into direct sunlight, he turned it over and discovered the secret. There was a tiny hole in the bottom which led to a second hole under the monkey's tail. "See," he told Tony, "when you pour in water it forces air up through this passage. There's your whistle."

"Crazy, man, crazy! Teach him to whistle 'La Cucaracha.' "

"I don't think any T-Town sharpie made *this* pot to sell *turistas*," Kern said.

Tony's face sobered. "Maybe you got something. Let's go ask an expert."

An expert here? Kern wondered. In La Ribera? But he trailed along with Tony down the road to a house near the beach. As soon as they entered he heard the creak of a wheel and soft slap-slap of hands—the sounds of a potter at work. Tony led the way to a patio where racks of clay vessels of every kind—bean pots, casseroles, dishes, and water jars—stood drying in the sun. A wizened birdlike woman sat under a ramada shaping a tall red vase on her kick wheel.

"This is Serafina," Tony said, "the village potmaker."

Glancing up, Serafina said, "Forgive me, *muchachos,* I cannot stop or I will lose the rhythm."

Fascinated, Kern watched the wet clay take form. Under her skilled hands it seemed to live and grow. Presently Serafina slowed the wheel with her foot, loosened the vase, and removed it to a drying board. Her pipestem arms were red to the elbow, as if dipped in paint.

78

"My friend also makes pots," Tony volunteered.

She eyed the bundle in Kern's hands. "So you come to learn Serafina's secrets?"

Kern blushed. "I am only a beginner, *Señora*, but I know it takes much strength to throw so large a vase. And you—"

"And I am a bundle of dried sticks." Serafina cackled and tapped her head. "But I have the knowledge here. This I also know: boys are always hungry."

She slipped away and returned with a plate of cakes and two glasses of raspberry-colored soda. While the boys ate she hopped about the patio showing her wares and chattering like a magpie. To his surprise Kern found that he could understand most of her rapid Spanish and ask a few comprehensible questions in return.

He did not ask about the whistling monkey, nor did Tony. That would be discourteous, an affront to hospitality. In her own good time Serafina would get around to it. And at last she did.

"But you did not come to hear an old woman gabble," she said. "What is it you are bursting to show me?"

Kern unwrapped the jug and handed it to her.

Serafina's eyes widened. She held the jug this way and that, making small clucking noises, then got a tiny pick from her tools and scratched delicately at the bottom. Kern exchanged a look with Tony and said, "Is it a fake, *Señora?*"

"The fakers are clever today," she said. "They mix lime and bone ash into their clay. When they fire a pot it makes a crust of green or red, to give the look of antiquity. No, this is no fake."

"Is it old?"

"Yes, very old."

"Perhaps a hundred years?"

Serafina smiled. "I am almost that old."

"Two hundred?"

"Older," Serafina said. "Before Columbus discovered the New World."

Kern sucked in his breath. 1492? Pre-Columbian? This jug he'd found in the brush, this monkey that could whistle, had been made at least five centuries ago!

CHAPTER 8

Bull was his usual grouchy self the following morning after breakfast. He looked red-eyed and rumpled, and chewed savagely on his toothpick. "Have any trouble yesterday?" he asked Kern.

"No," Kern said. "Why should I?"

"You didn't get much wood."

"Want me to haul another load?"

"Not today. Got another job for you." Bull led the way to one of the recovery rooms. The paint on one wall, a dull institutional gray, had been cracked in several places by a recent earthquake. "Strip her down and slap on another coat."

Kern moved the beds and cribs into the corridor, covered the floor with a spatter cloth, and attacked the wall with a wire brush and scraper. It was boring mechanical work, and when he was finally ready to paint an idea occurred to him. Old Sourpuss probably would say no, but it didn't cost anything to ask.

"Bull," he said. "Some of your recovery patients are kids, aren't they? Little kids?"

"Most of 'em."

"If you were sick, had to lie in bed day after day, wouldn't you get well quicker if you had something to look at besides an ugly gray wall?"

"What're you getting at, Dawson?"

"Let me jazz up that room while I'm at it. Wall murals."

"You an artist or something?"

It was the third time in two days he'd been asked that question. "That's right," Kern said. "A good one, too. Any objections?"

Bull surprised him with a grudging nod and went back to the dispensary. Kern unearthed a couple of Mexican comic books from the reception room, leafed through them for inspiration, and then remembered the jug. Why not? he thought with a grin. All kids liked monkeys. With a crayon he roughed out the scheme for his mural, got two cans of paint from the storeroom, and went to work.

Some while later, when he stepped down off the ladder, Kern discovered he had an audience of one. A small boy stood with his nose pressed against the window screen. It was Ramón, the boy who once had had a clubfoot. "Hi, Ramón," he called. "Where is your goat?"

For a moment he thought the boy was too shy to answer. Then Ramón said in a faltering voice, "He is at home, *Señor*."

"Did he haul water this morning?"

"Oh yes, many jars of water." Ramón stood on tiptoe and pointed. "That monkey, the fat one, his tail is too short."

82

Kern glanced up at the wall where half a dozen of his bright-red monkeys cavorted in a game of leapfrog. "You think it should be longer?"

Ramón nodded solemnly.

Kern backed off and narrowed his eyes, then nodded in agreement. "You're right. It lacks character." He dipped in his brush and with a flourish added a six-inch curl. "Better?"

"Yes, *Señor*." Ramón's eyes shone with silent laughter. "Now he is a true circus monkey." With that he ducked away from the window and vanished.

Appearing in the doorway, Bull said, "What was that all about?"

"I have a critic," Kern said.

Bull stared at the monkeys in silence, a bemused expression on his face, then shook his head and went away again.

Ramón returned that evening after supper while Kern was cleaning his brushes. This time he opened the conversation. "Please," he said, "will you show me how to paint a monkey?"

"I'm through painting for today, Ramón," Kern told him. "The wall's finished."

"Not on the wall." Ramón held out a scrap of paper. "Here."

With his pencil Kern quickly sketched a monkey and handed the paper back. "It's easy," he said. "Copy that until you can draw it freehand."

"But I do not wish always to draw monkeys."

Kern thought a moment. Whatever Ramón wanted, he was too proud and too polite to ask point blank. "A drawing lesson, is that what you want?"

Ramón's head bobbed emphatically.

Kern smothered a grin. Mr. Z., his art teacher back in Oceanview High, would never believe it. Leading Ramón to his room, he got out his drawing pad and pencils and dragged in an empty crate for a desk. "Let's start with something simple." He set a block of wood in the window ledge. "Don't draw yet, Ramón. Look at it first, very carefully."

Ramón stared at the block as though hypnotized.

"You see it with your eyes," Kern said. "But you must also see it with your brain, all of it, so that you can close your eyes and still see it. Do you understand?"

"*Si.* I must feel it inside."

"You'll know when you're ready. Take your time."

Ramón squeezed his eyes shut and opened them, drew a deep breath, and bent over the desk, his tongue curled over his upper lip. For several minutes the only sound was the soft friction of pencil lead against paper.

"Not bad," Kern said when he had finished. "It looks like wood. But hold your wrist like this." He slid an arm around Ramón's shoulder and guided his hand. "Now try again."

Ramón worked until the light began to fail, his face screwed up in total concentration, drawing the block over and over, and then an orange, the square shape and the round. The boy had an aptitude, Kern thought, perhaps real talent, and a lot of determination. "You come back tomorrow night, Ramón," he said, "and we'll have lesson number two."

"I would like that, *Señor,* but I cannot pay."

"You teach me Spanish. That's a fair trade."

Ramón's face brightened. "Do you think that someday I might become an artist?"

"If you work hard, and go to school."

"We have no school here."

"There's a school in Santa Ynez," Kern said. "Mama Rosa's kids go there."

"Ah, but she is Mama Rosa." Ramón seemed ill at ease, reluctant to say good night and go. Lingering in the doorway, he shifted from foot to foot, and Kern waited patiently until he blurted, "Can I see the real monkey, the one that whistles?"

"Where did you hear about that?"

"Everybody in the village knows."

"Who told you, Ramón?"

"I heard from my cousin Carlos, who heard from Jésus, who heard from Serafina herself."

Kern was beginning to realize that any incident in La Ribera was news, a morsel to be discussed at length and gossiped over. Still, he wished the old potmaker had not passed along the word. He brought the jug out from under his cot, made it whistle several times, much to Ramón's delight, and sent the boy home with his drawings.

As usual he had the clinic to himself at night. He prowled from room to room looking for a safer place to keep the jug and presently turned into the storeroom. Back in one corner Bull had stacked a number of hundred-pound bags of cement. He shifted them around until he'd formed a hollow in the middle, slipped the jug in, and re-covered the hole.

Nobody, he told himself, would ever think of looking there.

For the rest of the week Ramón came back every evening for his lesson. In return he drilled Kern in Spanish grammar and pronunciation. It helped pass the time at least. From scrap lumber Kern knocked together an easel, set it up behind the clinic, and during the long twilight hours taught Ramón a few fundamentals of water-color painting.

On his fourth visit Ramón brought his cousin Carlos and his friend Jésus, who stood in a silent attentive ring while Kern painted a village scene. They didn't ask to see the "Whistling Monkey," as he had come to think of the jug. Apparently they were curious about Kern himself, content to watch him work and then slip off as quietly as they had come. After that he had an audience every night.

On Saturday, which marked the end of Kern's second week at La Ribera, Bob Garth and his flying Buzzards failed to appear. He felt numb with disappointment. No mail, no word from home. Nothing to look forward to but the same old grind.

Late that afternoon, however, he had a visitor. He was washing the front windows when Hugo Hendryx drove up in his Land-Rover and climbed out. The resort owner mopped his moist round face with a handkerchief and shook hands. "Bull keeps you busy, I see," he said.

"Yes, sir," Kern said. "There's a lot to do around the place."

"The devil finds mischief for idle hands." Hendryx chuckled. "I have some news for you. About that truck driver."

"About Ricardo?"

"Whatever the name is. The one in the wreck." The Mexicali authorities, Hendryx said, had sent a radio message that Ricardo had been operated on successfully

86

and was now out of danger, but it would be some time before he could leave the hospital.

"Is he under arrest?"

"Arrest? Not that I know. Why, did he break some law?"

Kern sidestepped the question with a shrug. If Ricardo had been guilty of smuggling, or some other crime, the Mexican police would find out. His own suspicions were so vague he hadn't even mentioned them to Tony Vela.

"He probably overloaded his truck," Hendryx said. "But they all do that. Would you give the news to his family, if he has any?"

"Yes, sir. Thanks for your trouble, Mr. Hendryx."

"*Es nada.* Now then, I have a favor to ask you. I'd like to see your monkeys playing leapfrog."

Kern stared at him in confusion.

"Your painting on the wall." Hendryx smiled broadly. "The word has spread, you know. Can't hide your talents under a basket in this town."

Puzzled and self-conscious, Kern led him through the dispensary into the first recovery room. Hendryx took off his sun goggles and studied the mural of leaping monkeys. Without his glasses, Kern thought, the resort owner looked positively goggle-eyed, like some exotic fish hauled up from the deeps.

"Wonderful!" Hendryx chortled and wiped his eyes. "Oh, that's wonderful! Where'd you learn to paint like that?"

Here and there, Kern told him. At school. From his father. But mostly he'd taught himself.

"Can you paint fish?"

"Sure." He remembered his glass mosaic, the sketches he'd done at Sea World in San Diego, at the aquarium in La Jolla, the catches the sport-fishing fleet brought into Mission Bay. Fish? He could paint fish blindfold.

"How would you like to work for me, Kern?"

"I—I don't have much spare time."

"I mean full time," Hendryx said. "How much does Bull pay you?"

"Ten dollars."

"The old skinflint. I'll pay you fifty. Fifty dollars a week."

Kern blinked. He'd meant, of course, ten dollars a month. Hendryx was offering him two hundred, twenty times what the clinic paid, more than he'd earned all last summer mowing lawns.

"For a starter," Hendryx said, "there's my five guest cabins. And the lounge. You can paint the walls, marine stuff. And the boats. Everything needs a fresh coat. This climate's murder on paint."

"You'll pay me fifty dollars a week—just to paint?"

"There'll be other work when the season starts. Right now I have to get La Serenidad in shape. Cost me a mint to hire a painter from the States."

"I—I don't know, Mr. Hendryx. It sounds great, but—"

"No hurry. Think it over. Take your time." Hendryx' eyes disappeared behind the sun goggles and he walked back out to his Rover. "Where's Bull?" he asked.

"Around somewhere, I guess," Kern said. "He usually goes fishing about now."

"Fishing, eh? Well, I hope he won't take it hard if you decide to switch jobs. Serve him right, the tightwad."

Open-mouthed, Kern watched him drive away in a cloud of dust. A job! he thought. A real job, for real money, out of the blue, the last thing he'd ever expected. No more hauling water and emptying slop jars? No more of this gung-ho, spit-'n'-polish routine? No more reveille? No more Bull Kalinski? It sounded too good to be true.

The hitch was, Kern realized, he'd made a deal with Bob Garth. He'd have to square it with Garth first.

Bull came out from Mama Rosa's house chewing on a toothpick and stared after the Land-Rover. "What did Hendryx want?" Bull said. "Free bellyache pills?"

Kern gave him the message about Ricardo. He didn't mention the job.

"So Ricardo pulled through," Bull said. "That's good."

"Mr. Hendryx asked me to tell his family."

"He doesn't have any family here. What else did Fish Face say?"

"Nothing," Kern said. "You don't like him, do you?"

Bull grinned crookedly. "Now whatever gave you that notion?" He started for the door, then turned back, his face stern once more. "Don't mess with that guy, Dawson. He's trouble."

What kind of trouble, Kern wanted to ask, but knew he'd get no answer from Bull. "Tomorrow's Sunday," he said. "Am I still on restriction?"

"You're restricted seven days a week, till I tell you diff'rent."

Nuts to you, buddy, Kern thought a few minutes later, as Bull went marching down the road with his rod and tackle box. Go take a running jump in the Gulf, Kalinksi. I'm not your slave. Not any more.

He waited until he saw Bull take off from the anchorage in the skiff, then got his jacket and a flashlight from his room, and walked through the village to the waterfront. Nobody answered his knock at the house Tony Vela had pointed out, but he found Tony himself at the dock with several other fishermen. He knew one or two by name now, those who had come to the clinic, and he nodded and got a smile in return.

Tony grinned hello and said, "How's the art teacher?"

"I'll swap you for that course in five easy lessons," Kern said. "Can you latch onto a boat tonight?"

"*Si*. But fishing's better in the morning."

"This fish bites after sundown."

"Oh-ho!" Tony whistled softly. "Checking on El Toro?"

Kern peered out across the Gulf, whose surface looked almost blood red in the rays of the setting sun. He understood now why, among other names, the early Spaniards had called it the Vermilion Sea. Bull's skiff was a rapidly dwindling speck against the horizon. "That's the general idea. Can do?"

Tony's eyes lighted up. "Can do, man. Be my guest. Just one problem."

"What?"

"What do we tell *los pescadores?*" Tony indicated the group of fishermen who stood nearby, smoking their cornhusk cigarettes and eying the boys with curiosity. "Only a nut goes out at night. They'll talk."

Kern pondered. "Tell 'em I want to paint the sea by moonlight. Everybody knows artists are crazy."

CHAPTER 9

El Bobo was an old but durable-looking boat sixteen feet long with an inboard motor and decking over the bow. It belonged to his grandfather, Tony explained, and could make up to eight knots in a calm sea. From it the men of the Vela family earned their living by fishing.

The boys loaded an extra can of fuel aboard, and while Tony warmed up the motor Kern cast off the lines. The red tide had drifted away and the water was clear, revealing a smooth sandy bottom. As they chugged away from the anchorage and headed out for open sea, *Bobo* began to roll. Breathing gasoline fumes and ancient fish, Kern had an unhappy thought: What if I get seasick?

Tony steered a course for the point and the familiar outline of La Ribera fell astern, dwarfed by the encircling hills. A light evening breeze sprang up, ruffling the surface and dashing dollops of spray over the gunwales. Kern zipped up his jacket and peered ahead for a glimpse of Bull's skiff, amazed to find how vast and empty the Gulf seemed this close to shore. "Bull has a long head start," he said. "What if we don't spot him before dark?"

"No sweat, man. I got X-ray eyes."

"What's he got against Hendryx, the fellow who owns Serenidad?"

Tony shrugged. "Bull's one hard gringo to figure. He's a loner, doesn't make friends."

"He's pretty chummy with Mama Rosa."

"Everybody's nice to Mama Rosa. They feel sorry for her." Some time ago, Tony related, Mama Rosa's husband had been caught on the Gulf by a *chubasco,* a violent storm. He'd washed overboard and drowned. The tragedy had left her a widow with five small children to raise.

"Oh," Kern said, and felt his cheeks grow warm. He wished he knew more about all these villagers, about Mama Rosa and Ramón and Serafina and Tony himself. They didn't complain. They kept their troubles to themselves. Even Bull Kalinski, Kern admitted. After two weeks he knew almost nothing about the ex-Marine.

As the sky darkened and the air cooled, the breeze shifted around to the west, blowing from the mountains. Presently Tony neared the headland and throttled down, altered course, and cruised slowly under tall cliffs. Silent and intent, his yachtsman's cap tilted at a rakish angle, he skirted the rocks and scanned the waters ahead for what he called a "hotspot," a school of fish forced to the surface by sharks or porpoises or other hungry foragers. Suddenly he pointed and reduced speed still more.

In the fading light Kern made out a patch of sea that looked aboil, lashed into tiny white waves by slashing

92

fins. Overhead a cloud of birds squawked and screamed as they circled the frantic fish. Gulls, terns, cormorants, a dozen varieties he had never seen before, struggled to get in on the feast. "Watch this," Tony said.

A dark-legged, awkward-looking bird skimmed low and smacked the water, then soared aloft with a wriggling fish in its beak. Instantly a second bird, a huge coal-black creature with scarlet throat pouch, swooped on the first in a murderous dive. The smaller bird plunged back into the sea and submerged until the attacker flew off, then surfaced with its prize intact.

Tony laughed. "That's *el bobo*. Booby bird. Outsmarts a frigate bird every time. Now you see how we named the boat."

"Let's hope Bull doesn't booby-trap us tonight," Kern said.

The hotspot subsided as abruptly as it had appeared, leaving the sea glassy smooth, and the hordes of birds grew silent and began to scatter. Tony killed the motor and tossed out the anchor. He got a long-handled net, made a couple of dips over the stern, and dumped several small silvery fish into the live-bait tank. "Anchovies," he said. "We better make this look for real in case our boy gets curious. Don't want to scare him off."

"Where do you think he is?"

"Cozied up in some cove, waiting for dark."

"We could be wrong, Tony. I've seen some diehard fishing buffs."

"But six nights a week? No, El Toro's up to something." Tony handed him a stubby cane rod and reel, bent on a sinker, and showed him how to fasten the bait on the hook. With misgivings Kern stood up, braced himself, and cast the way he'd seen surf fishermen do. Too late, Tony yelled, "Hey, not so hard!"

The line arched out, looped back, and wound itself around the rod in a horrendous tangle. Tony shook with laughter. "Backlash," he chortled. "That's not a baseball bat, man. Easy does it."

Disgruntled and angry, mostly at himself, Kern worked out the snarls, then watched Tony demonstrate a time or two, and tried again. On his fourth cast he managed to drop his bait a respectable distance from the boat and let it sink to the bottom. Within seconds he felt a tug and jerked hard on the rod, but the tension slacked off. Tony tested the line and shook his head. "Let him swallow the bait before you set the hook."

Laboriously Kern reeled in, put on another anchovy, and cast again. This time, after a brief but furious struggle, he hoisted a tawny spotted fish alongside, where Tony gaffed and pulled it aboard. "Leopard grouper," Tony said. "Weigh a good ten pounds. I'll make a fisherman outa you yet."

Within the next hour Kern hooked seven more fish, four of which he lost and three which he boated—two spotted bass and another grouper. Then they suddenly stopped biting. Even so, he had to agree that the Gulf must be an angler's paradise. "Back home," he told Tony, "I've seen guys fish for hours without a single strike."

"Beginner's luck." Tony cocked an eye at the star-sprinkled sky. "Haul in your line. We may have to move out fast."

In his excitement Kern had forgotten the purpose of

their trip, nor had he been aware of night closing in. He put away his tackle, wiped the scales off his hands, and settled in the stern. The breeze had freshened and little waves slapped against the hull. Her planking creaking softly, *Bobo* rode the sea like a cork. Once he jumped when a sea lion barked somewhere under the cliffs. He felt cold and cramped now, and his stomach was queasy from the constant motion.

"Hear anything?" Tony said.

Kern listened to the sea sighing over the rocks. This is a wild-goose chase, he told himself. We're the nuts, not Bull, sitting out here in the dark like a pair of corny TV agents. Waiting for what? But I can't back out now. I talked Tony into this.

Tony's voice dropped to a whisper. "We got company."

Kern peered over the side. A bottlenose dolphin had risen behind the boat, its sleek hide glistening in the starlight. For a moment it seemed suspended there, inspecting the boys placidly, its clown's mouth stretched in a smile, then sank without a ripple.

Immediately Kern felt better. "Are dolphins as smart as people say?"

"Smarter," Tony said. "They have built-in sonar. We could use one tonight."

"Tony, how long would it take a fast boat to cross from the mainland?"

"Four, five hours. Depends where you start from, how much head wind you have to buck."

"Could you hide a boat on this side during the day, then cross back the next night?"

"You'd have to know this coast like a *vagabundo*."

95

"*Vagabundo?*"

"Sea gypsy. They sail up and down in dugout canoes." Tony put a finger to his lips. "Listen!"

Kern raised his head, hearing only the slosh of water under the keel; then the wind veered and carried to his ears the faint throb of an engine. It came from the east, the seaward side, near the end of the point, growing steadily weaker until it faded altogether. "That's an outboard, maybe forty horse. No big power job." Tony said.

"How can you tell?"

"After a while you develop an ear. He's heading out."

Tony signaled him to hoist anchor and started the motor. *Bobo* glided from under the cliffs and began to pitch as soon as they left the protection of the point. Kern could see no sign of a boat anywhere, but Tony opened up to full power and held to a steady course with apparent unconcern. East, due east, Kern determined, after locating Polaris. Was Bull heading for a rendezvous at sea?

For some distance the dolphin swam alongside, cavorting like some playful escort, then dove across the bow and went its separate way. The wind freshened at their backs, pushing the boat through choppy waves. Now and then she took one head on, and Kern got busy with the bailing can. They cleared the headland, and after a mile or so Tony cut the motor and stood up with his hands cupped behind his ears. "Wind's blowing the wrong way," he said.

Kern strained forward, peering into the night. Maybe, he thought, Bull had killed his motor, too, and was listening for them. Then he heard a barely audible pulse of sound. Tony nodded. "That's him. He's changed course."

How Tony could be so positive Kern didn't know, but he set off again, altering direction to the northeast. Spray whipped in from the port side now, drenching them to the skin. The racket of the motor throbbed against Kern's eardrums and his teeth began to chatter. They had to be right about one thing, he decided: No man, not even Bull Kalinski, would bounce around out here in the dark and wet and cold just to catch a few fish.

Twice more Tony stopped to listen, and both times picked up the sound of the other boat, although Kern heard nothing. But on the fourth stop they drew a blank. For several minutes Tony sat drifting in silence, turning his head this way and that, trying to detect some vibration in the air. Then he lay down and pressed his ear against the floorboards. "Sometimes you can hear a prop a long way off," he said. "But no dice tonight. We lost him."

"You think he knew he was being followed?" Kern asked.

"Could be he doubled back to throw us off."

Kern stared back at the distant shoreline, surprised how far they had come from La Ribera. No glow of village lights was visible, only the black silhouette of mountains.

"I gotta hunch, though," Tony said, "that he outran us. Every time we stopped he opened up a bigger lead."

"Tony, would he meet a boat at sea, without lights? Unless he's a hotshot navigator?"

Tony said nothing for a minute, then snapped his fingers. *"Olé!* If he's making for a landfall the only land out here—" Tony pointed over the starboard bow. "Isla Lagarto."

Kern remembered the island he had noticed from the beach the day he'd gone to gather firewood for Mama Rosa, an island with a jagged spine that suggested a prehistoric lizard. From this angle and distance—about three miles, he judged—it looked uninviting if not downright sinister, with high bluffs and a fringe of giant offshore rocks. "Anybody live there?"

"Two million seagulls," Tony said.

"You ever been ashore?"

"No, but there's s'posed to be places a guy can land."

Kern glanced at his watch. Eleven-thirty, much later than he'd thought. Tomorrow he'd be dead on his feet, but he might not have this chance again. "Let's take a quick look before we head back."

Running at full throttle, the boys closed on Lizard Island, then Tony slowed to quarter speed and worked *Bobo* in cautiously through the shoals. Cliffs pitted with huge caves rose sheer from the water line. The sea surged in and out, foaming over rocks and ledges and tugging at the boat as if to suck her under. Kern's muscles tightened as he thought of whirlpools. Not that he believed in whirlpools—not in sea monsters either—but he had the spooky feeling that anything could happen here.

Hunting for a break in the island's western wall, they nosed ahead and shortly sighted an indentation. Tony maneuvered through a narrow channel at the base of the cliffs into a small cove, a cove empty of boats. With a mixture of disappointment and relief, Kern hopped out on the black shingle beach and made the line fast around a boulder. Obviously he and Tony had guessed wrong about Bull's destination, but it was a pleasure to plant his feet on firm ground again. He stared up at the dark rims and said, "We might be able to see the other side from on top."

"Bad place to get caught if the wind picks up," Tony said.

"Fifteen minutes? That should do it."

"Okay. But don't blame me if we have to sit out a blow."

Kern checked his flashlight and took the lead as they scrambled up from the beach over steep slippery rocks. Loose stones clattered underfoot and startled birds, disturbed at their rest, squawked in protest. The crests on either side, white with guano, stood out against the night sky like snowy mounds. From the top of the cove a gully angled sharply up to their left and led into the saddle of a low ridge.

Huddled in the lee of a boulder, the boys caught their breath as they looked down at the far side of Lizard Island. The portion they could see was less precipitous than the western face, dropping off to the Gulf in a maze of canyons and arroyos. A single peak, the Lizard's "horn," dominated the north end. But nowhere along that rugged coastline did there appear to be another cove or beach where a boat could land safely.

Some distance down the back slope Kern made out a faint threadlike scar among the black volcanic rock. "Looks like a trail."

"Could be some *javelinas* here," Tony said. "Wild pigs."

Kern switched on his light and played the beam back and forth. "Then there has to be fresh water. A spring."

"I'll ask my grandfather. He knows—"

There was a sudden angry whine and rock splattered behind Kern's head. Then came the hum of a ricochet, followed by the delayed K-A-W-H-O-O-M! of a rifle.

Kern froze in place, his throat constricted. The flashlight slithered out of his grasp with a tinkle of shattered glass. Beside him Tony stood like stone. K-A-W-H-O-O-M! the rifle crashed again in the teeth of the wind. The rolling echo of the second shot jarred Kern out of his trance. He grabbed Tony's arm and pulled him down. After a tension-wracked silence they crawled behind the boulder.

"He—he's shooting at us!" Tony whispered in a tone of disbelief.

"Somebody sure is. That was close." Now that his initial shock had worn off, Kern was beginning to think more clearly. Whoever the somebody was, he had been alerted by the light. Very possibly he would shoot again or come hunting them. And, most important—where was he now? What was he doing? The why and the how of it had to wait. "You see anything?"

Tony raised his head a fraction of an inch. "Black as a bat down there."

From the sound alone it was impossible to tell how far away, or how near, the man had been when he fired, but there was no doubt the wind direction gave him a tremendous advantage. Also, he must know the island. Should they yell at him, demand an explanation? That would be the normal thing to do. No, Kern thought. Don't give him any more of a target to shoot at. Clear out. Fast.

"Come on!"

On their stomachs the boys wormed down off the saddle. Once they had the ridge at their backs they jumped to their feet and ran down the gully, hurdling rocks and holes in a dash for the boat. Kern tripped and fell, banging his knee, then sprang up and raced after Tony. The wind had grown steadily in strength, and now it met them head on as it whistled up the draw. Tony's cap sailed off his head and went skimming into space. Tears streamed from Kern's eyes, but he stumbled on blindly.

When they broke into the open at the top of the cove the wind hit them with battering force, as though trying to drive them back. Bent almost double, they fought their way to the edge and, slipping and sliding, climbed down to the beach. Tony vaulted into the boat and Kern ran to free the mooring line.

He heard Tony's muffled shout and whirled around. Tony was staring out at the channel mouth, now transformed into a caldron of seething white water. Great windswept combers pounded through the opening, slammed into the cove, and exploded against the rocks with a deafening boom. Spray hung in a fine dense mist that curtained off the Gulf.

"Can you take her out through this?" Kern yelled.

"*Dios!* The first wave'd swamp us."

The cliffs behind drew Kern's eye like a magnet. Tony had tried to warn him. But he'd been too stubborn to listen. *Fifteen minutes should do it.* So now, thanks to him, they were trapped on Lizard Island, trapped between the sea and a screwball with a rifle.

CHAPTER 10

Tony shouted at him again, but the howl of the wind and the crash of waves drowned out his voice. How far behind them was the man? Straining to penetrate the darkness, Kern swept his gaze along the upper rim. Not in sight yet. But any minute, any second, he might appear. There seemed no other way to climb out. Sitting ducks they were, penned in to a tiny shelf of beach.

Then Tony was beside him, tugging at his arm. "Hide! We gotta hide!"

"Where?"

With water washing around their ankles they slogged along the narrow strip of shingle, but after a few yards it pinched out against a sheer unclimbable wall. They reversed their steps and waded back past *Bobo,* which now wallowed helplessly in the rising sea. Kern had a bitter moment of remorse. This was the Vela family boat, the source of their livelihood. If the line broke, or she smashed on the shoals—

The cove curved around to the left and here, too, the beach ended against a cliff, but the sea had carved out a series of potholes. Kern leaned far out, trying to see if they offered an escape, but a bulge of rock cut off his view. With one more upward glance at the rims, he motioned Tony to wait and tested the nearest hole for footing. It held. He kicked off his shoes and tied them around his neck and, with his bare toes gripping, edged along the base of the cliff.

Spread-eagled against the rock, he found his balance and worked forward cautiously, feeling for handholds. One big wave burst against his legs and almost tore him loose, but he managed to hang on and after a moment, resumed his crablike progress. Don't look down, Dawson, he told himself. Think positive. You can make it, you have to make it. You want a rifle slug in your back?

He inched around the bulge, fighting a panicky urge to hurry, and nearly skidded off into an inky bottomless-looking pool. Smooth hundred-foot cliffs enclosed it on three sides. Kern stared in dismay. Not even a lizard—if there were a lizard on this island—could climb any farther. But some twenty yards across the pool he made out a hole; not a pothole, but a genuine cave-size hole, big enough to admit a man, or maybe a couple of boys.

Creeping back to the bulge, he signaled frantically and waited in an agony of suspense while Tony negotiated the slippery crossing and rejoined him. "Cave," he said. "Have to swim for it."

Tony's lips moved soundlessly and he crossed himself.

Kern lowered himself into the pool, drew a lungful

of air, and shoved off, before he could think about any slimy creature that might be lurking in the depths. Waves pummeled him in relays, small angry waves spending their last strength before dashing against the rocks. Battling the undertow created by their backlash, he stroked furiously into calmer water and crawled out panting into the cave mouth. Seconds later Tony splashed up beside him.

Together they peered into the opening, a scallop-edged hole head high and about three feet wide. A dank iodine smell wafted out of the charcoal blackness. The boys looked at each other. "High tide?" Kern asked.

"Doubt it," Tony said. "May go higher."

Kern knew that the head of the Gulf, where it received the discharge of the Colorado River, had one of the highest tides in the world. Sometimes it dropped ten feet in as many minutes. A ten-foot rise would drown them like rats. "How much higher?"

"Dunno. I'll chance it if you will."

Kern thrust out his arms in front of his face and stepped gingerly into the cave, feeling his way in knee-deep water. The floor was level for a short distance, then he stumbled into a hole and the sea whirled around his waist. When he stopped, Tony collided against him from behind. Feet braced and teeth clenched, he listened to the drip of water in the darkness ahead. Something slithered against his calf and twined around his legs. Petrified with fear, he thought: Jellyfish tentacles? Octopus? Moray eel?

"Sea grass," Tony said, as if reading his mind. "Man, I nearly jumped through the roof."

Kern gave a shaky laugh to cover his relief, untangled himself, and waded on to the far side of the hole. Here the cave made a turning and he bumped his head on the ceiling as he groped around the corner. The cave, like the beach outside, was squeezing in to a dead end. If we had just one dry match between us, he thought. Ducking low, he willed himself to take another step, and another. Then he banged against more rock, solid rock. Exploring with his fingertips, he traced the outline of a hollow about shoulder high, above the water level. He hauled himself up, discovered room enough for a precarious perch, and gave Tony a hand.

In wet silent misery they huddled in their niche, hugging their knees for warmth. Moisture oozed from the roof in a slow steady rhythm and dripped down the back of their necks. The noise of the storm outside was muted, but at their feet the unseen waters gurgled ominously. Any moment Kern expected the glow of a light to emerge around the bend, searching them out, but as the minutes passed another thought occurred to him: The man with the rifle wouldn't risk drowning in a cave. He'd wait for them to come out.

"Tide's still rising," Tony said.

Kern speared one leg over the ledge as a measuring rod and felt the sea lap at his instep. It seemed only seconds before the level had crept up to his ankle. He tried to judge how much headroom they had left. Maybe three feet. "Moon's on the wane tonight. Does that prove anything?"

"Not in the Gulf. We got everything. *Marea muerta,* underwater currents, waterspouts, even tidal waves."

"*Muerta* which?"

"Dead tide. That's what the pirates used to call it."

The walls of the cave distorted their voices like an

105

echo chamber. Kern shifted position and tested the level with his other leg. It had risen to mid-shin. Then it was at his kneecap. At this rate it would reach the roof in minutes. He had to get his mind on something else. "Tony?"

"*Si?*"

"Do you ever think about the future?"

"Heaven, you mean?"

"Are you going back to school someday? Maybe get a job?"

"I got a job, *hijo*. My grandfather says: No work, no eat. So I catch fish."

"You want to be a fisherman always?"

"Ha! Every kid in Mexico wants to fight the bulls. That's me, matador."

"Have you ever fought a bull?"

"I can dream, can't I?" What he really wanted, Tony said, was to save his money and buy a fishing boat, a big twin-screw cruiser. Then he'd go in the *turista* business like *Señor* Hendryx and take out rich Americans like his friend Kern Dawson.

Kern found he was actually grinning. "That's all we both need—money."

"So we catch this smuggler and collect a big fat reward." After a long silence Tony added, "It's stopped, I think."

Kern touched his kneecap. Had the water risen higher, perhaps half an inch? He couldn't be sure. Holding his body rigid, he concentrated on the muffled roar of surf against the rocks outside. Had it changed ever so slightly, become less violent? Imagination, he told himself. But now his whole knee was exposed. Then his upper shinbone. The tide had turned!

"Santa Maria!" Tony breathed. "Now I believe in miracles."

Kern was so limp he could only let out a long wavering sigh.

After that he alternately dozed and stared into the darkness, head bobbing on his chest. The hands of his illuminated watch had stopped at twelve-thirty-five; evidently moisture had seeped through the "moisture proof" case. The tide had dropped below the level of their feet, but he and Tony decided they wouldn't attempt to leave before daybreak. In the cave they were safe for now. Somehow the hours dragged by.

Half asleep he gave a start when Tony nudged him with an elbow. "What?" he mumbled.

"Time to go."

Kern jerked awake and opened his eyes. The rumble of the sea had quieted and a feeble light had crept into the cave, blotching the walls with greenish shadows that looked like mildew. Rubbery heaps of seaweed left by the ebbing tide covered the floor below. He stretched his legs and slid down from the ledge. A hermit crab scuttled into a crack and kelp balls squished soggily under his feet. It was astounding how harmless and commonplace all this seemed in daylight.

"I'll bet our friend gave up hours ago," he said.

"You hope," Tony said. "No telling what that nut'll do."

Kern picked his way along the edge of the tide pools where the cave made its bend. In an instant his new-found confidence crumbled like sand. His heart hammering wildly, he flattened against the wall and waved Tony back. From beyond the turn came the unmistakable sound of heavy breathing. Their man had waited for daylight, too, Kern thought. And now he was here, just around the corner.

Water splashed. Then silence. Kern reached down for a rock to use as a weapon and came up with a handful of pebbles. The breathing resumed, a rapid and asthmatic wheezing that goose-pimpled his skin. Another splash, closer this time. He held his breath and crouched, ready to spring.

Suddenly a brown bewhiskered snout poked into view. A sea lion pup waddled onto a rock, balanced on its front flippers, and sniffed the air. For a second they stared at each other in mutual amazement. Then, with a snort, the sea lion flipped around and retreated.

Kern straightened slowly and let his pebbles drop. With a sheepish grin at Tony, he crowed like a rooster.

Tony laughed. "Lead on, Brother Chicken. Let's bug outa here."

The boys waded across the last big pool, now only knee deep, and walked to the mouth of the cave. Blinking at the sunlight, they stared out into a world totally different from that of the night before, a world of calm sea and pearly sky. A single puff of cloud hovered on the horizon and swarms of fish-hunting birds soared and circled above the cove. "They wouldn't be up like that," Kern said, "if a man was hiding in the cliffs."

"One way to find out."

Boldly Tony stepped out into the open and peered up at the rims, as though defying anyone to challenge him. Kern swallowed and stepped out beside him. The birds took alarm, mewing and scolding raucously over this invasion of their domain, and melted away. Reassured, the boys climbed back over the rocks and found *Bobo* secure at her mooring, apparently none the worse from the blow. They searched up and down the beach but turned up nothing to indicate that a visitor had been there during their absence.

"We could take another look on top," Kern said.

"And get shot at again?" Tony demanded. "Next time he might not miss."

"Somehow I can't believe it was Bull."

"He was a sharpshooter in the Marines. I saw his medals once."

That didn't make Bull a smuggler, Kern reflected. They still needed proof. But one fact they had learned: Strangers weren't welcome on Lizard Island. I'm coming back, he promised himself; someday I'm coming back and search the whole place.

The motor coughed and sputtered but caught on the fourth try. Tony took *Bobo* out through the narrows and set a course for La Ribera. As the island receded over the stern, Kern kept watch for a boat or a trace of smoke or even a tiny human figure on the cliffs, but there was only lifeless black rock thrusting out of the sea. Isla Lagarto had kept its secret.

Their own secret, the boys agreed, should be kept between themselves, for the present anyway. Nobody had to know about the shooting. If his grandfather found out, Tony said, there would be no more night trips in *Bobo*.

About midmorning they coasted into the village anchorage and made fast. A few of the ever-present *pescadores* lounging about the dock watched them unload and grinned knowingly at the skimpy catch of fish Kern lugged ashore. A week ago he would have bristled, but now he grinned back. Tony tapped his shoulder and said, "El Toro beat us in."

"You sure?"

Tony pointed out a gray skiff drawn up on the beach and chained to an iron stake. "I wonder how long ago."

The skiff looked like Bull somehow, Kern thought. Neat, shipshape, blunt nosed, with its outboard hooded in a canvas jacket. Old Blood 'n' Guts. And now he had to face the man. "Wish me luck."

"Want me to come with you?" Tony asked.

Kern shook his head. "Thanks. I've been chewed out before. By pros. See ya, Tony."

"See ya, man."

He was conscious of Tony's stare on his back as he plodded wearily up the street. Tony knew. Job or no job, he *was* afraid of Bull. Not only had he disobeyed Bull's orders; he'd followed him, tried to spy on him. The question was: Did Bull know that?

As the dust squirted up between his bare toes, Kern remembered, belatedly, one other item. Sometime during the night he'd lost his shoes, the same blue tennies that had led to his downfall back in Oceanview. Except for those tennies he'd be home right now, mowing lawns or bagging groceries at the supermarket, no troubles on his mind. Maybe that was some kind of omen. But was it good? Or bad?

He had a dim hope that Bull had not come directly from the landing to the clinic. He just might be able to sneak in and fake it that he'd been there all the time. But the jeep was parked in front. Last evening Bull had left it out behind. Squaring his shoulders, Kern stepped through the door.

110

CHAPTER   11

A tall thin man with crew-cut hair and horn-rim glasses peered up at Kern from the reception desk. *"Hola, amigo!"*

Kern stared. "Mr. Garth!"

"Doctor Howard and I flew down for the day. We just got in," Bob Garth said. "How are you getting along?"

"All right," Kern said. If he hadn't been so worried he would have noticed the plane on the landing strip. "Have you seen Bull?"

"He met us in the jeep." The Spanish teacher regarded him with a dry smile. "Two weeks and your mother wouldn't recognize you."

Kern colored, suddenly aware of his bedraggled appearance—the ratty old hat Garth had given him, the dried fish blood on his shirt, the knee rip in his jeans. He might have told Garth the whole story then, about the shooting and the mysterious boat at night, but Bull appeared in the doorway. He gave Kern a flat searching stare and said, "Kind of late getting to work, aren't you, Dawson?"

"Never mind that now," Garth said. "I saw your folks last night, Kern. They sent their love. Also some mail." He held out several envelopes and a package. "We'll talk after you've had a chance to read it."

Granted a reprieve, Kern hurried through the dispensary, where Dr. Howard looked up with an absent-minded nod, and back to his room. Closing his door, he opened the package first. It contained three layers of brownies, "baked by my own lily white hands," his sister Beth had written. Also a cartoon picture of himself sprawled in a hammock with a guitar, above the caption "You lucky bum."

Two of the letters were from his mother. Mrs. Dawson was concerned that he might not be eating the proper food and whether he had enough clothes. She reminded him to be careful of rattlesnakes. The third letter was, unexpectedly, from his father. Sam Dawson had landed a part-time job in an Oceanview department store, and rented a room near the family duplex. Kern read over the last two lines: "I hope by now, son, that you've discovered you made the right choice. But right or wrong you made it yourself, and that's what counts."

He got out his pen and stationery and started to reply, but fell asleep in the middle of the first sentence.

A tap on the door awakened him much later, and Bob Garth came in. "We're taking off in a few minutes," Garth said. "Do I win my bet?"

Kern knuckled the sleep from his eyes. "What bet?"

"Your old friend Clark Stover, the boys' veepee, bet me five dollars you wouldn't stick it out."

"You mean it's up to me?" Kern asked. "What's Bull say?"

"Bull says, quote: 'I wish I had that censored kid in my old training platoon at Pendleton for one censored day.'"

It sounded so exactly like Bull that Kern had to grin. "Didn't he squawk about last night?"

"No. Should he?"

Now was the time to spill it all, Kern thought, beginning with the truck wreck. Maybe he and Tony needed some adult advice. But did they know enough yet to ask for help? Could be, but not enough to lower the boom on Bull. Without proof, Garth would take Bull's side, and that would end the ball game. Besides, he might get Tony in trouble.

"Bull and I had a hassle last week," he said, "and he restricted me. Last night I took off fishing."

Garth's attention had strayed to the wall calendar on which Kern had crossed off every day but one of his stay in La Ribera. "Prisoner of Devil's Island," Garth said. "Is it that bad?"

"I'll stay," Kern said. Somehow this decision had made itself without conscious effort on his part. "If you want me."

"Good boy." Garth clapped him on the shoulder. "You and Bull fight your own battles. Maybe you'll win the war."

Kern hesitated. He knew he should ask Garth about

the job Hugo Hendryx had offered him at the fishing resort, for fifty dollars a week. Garth could hardly refuse him a chance like that. But again, something held him back. If I quit the clinic now, he thought, I won't be able to keep an eye on Bull; I'll never find out what his racket is.

"Well, that's settled," Garth said. "I'll tell your mother you're not starving. Any last requests?"

Kern started to say no, then he thought of the Whistling Monkey. "Next time you come could you bring me a book from the library, a book on pre-Columbian art?" From memory he quickly drew a sketch of the monkey jug. "Stuff like this."

Garth studied it, then gave Kern a quizzical look. "Any special reason?"

"Nooo. Guess I just like monkeys."

"So do I," Garth said. "Even on murals, I'll see what I can dig up."

Later, Kern rode out in the jeep to the airstrip with him and Dr. Howard and Bull. As the engines warmed up, billowing dust across the field, he had a last-minute doubt. I still can change my mind, he thought. Four hours from now I can be home. La Ribera, so long! But then what?

The plane taxied into the wind and took off, circled the village once for altitude, and dwindled into the north. He watched until it disappeared. Then he swung around to face Bull, knowing there would be no escape this time.

"So you went over the hill last night," Bull said, in a flat toneless voice. "A.W.O.L."

"Go ahead, sergeant, blow your whistle."

"I could've shipped you out with Garth just now."

"Why didn't you?"

"Don't think I wasn't tempted. Where'd you go?"

"Fishing. We got caught in that storm, Tony Vela and I. Couldn't launch his boat till the wind died."

"Caught where?" Bull said.

"Some island. Ask Tony, he'll tell you."

"Whose idea was it? Vela's?"

"Mine," Kern said. "So what happens now—you throw me in the brig?"

Bull stared him up and down, and for an instant Kern thought he'd pushed him too far. But Bull shook his head and said, "Why don't you grow up, Dawson? We got a job to do. Knock that chip off your shoulder."

"Am I still restricted?"

"Negative." Bull about-faced and climbed into the jeep.

Open-mouthed with surprise, Kern slid in beside him. Will the real Bull Kalinski please stand up, he thought. What gives? Why hadn't Bull reported him to Garth? He'd threatened to often enough. And then a possible reason occurred to him. Bull thinks I know too much; he's making a deal: *You keep your mouth shut, I'll keep mine shut.* A kind of armed truce.

Next morning brought another surprise. After breakfast Bull announced that he had to make a business trip up the coast. He would take the jeep and be gone two nights, perhaps longer, leaving Kern in charge of the clinic.

"Business trip?" Kern said.

"Business." Bull did not elaborate. "Think you can manage on your own?"

"If nobody gets sick."

"You've had a First Aid course, haven't you? That's all we can handle anyway. There's a medical handbook in the office. If an emergency comes up, get Hendryx to radio for help."

By seven o'clock Bull had gassed up and driven off, after loading several packages of assorted sizes into the jeep. Kern waited until his dust had settled and hurried back to Bull's room. For one thing, he wanted to see if Bull owned a rifle. Also he was curious about the packages. The door was locked, secured by a sturdy new-looking padlock. Kern tried the windows, but both were fastened tight and curtained with some opaque material. *Bull's a loner,* Tony Vela had said. That might explain the lock, but not this sudden mysterious trip over Smugglers' Road.

It was pleasant, however, to be his own boss for a change, to work without Bull breathing down his neck. Only one patient came in during the morning, a small girl who had scratched her arm. Kern swabbed the cut with Merthiolate and sent her home with a pack of chewing gum. A second patient appeared after lunch, an old man complaining of an earache. Kern explained that he would have to wait until a doctor arrived, probably next Saturday. Meanwhile he could only prescribe aspirin to ease the pain.

At five o'clock he finished the last of his chores for the day and hurried down to the beach. Bull's absence had one other advantage: He and Tony could take their time exploring Lizard Island, and this time they'd go prepared. But *Bobo* was not at her mooring. Tony, he learned from one of the fishermen, had left at daybreak with his grandfather in pursuit of a school of albacore. When would they be back? The fisherman shrugged, as if only a gringo would ask such a foolish question.

Kern gazed off at the haze-shrouded island and walked slowly back to the clinic.

Two saddled horses stood beside the road and a man was squatting in the shade under the red-cross sign. He wore leather chaps, and as he rose to his feet Kern saw the weariness in his face and had an instant premonition of trouble. It was the ranchero, the one called Luis, who had brought them news of the truck accident.

"Señor," Luis said, "where is El Toro?"

"El Toro left this morning," Kern said. "For several days."

The ranchero rubbed an arm across his eyes as though warding off a blow. "That is bad. Very bad."

"Can I help you?"

"Can you ride a horse?"

Kern glanced at the two scrubby brown animals, who looked as tired as their owner. *"Poco.* A little."

"Then you must come with me. My brother has been hurt." Luis spoke in bursts, like a long-distance runner at the end of a race. Two weeks ago, he said, his brother José had ridden into the mountains to search for feed for their cattle. When he failed to return, Luis became worried and went to look for him. At their line camp he had found José unconscious, weak from loss of blood with a wound in his thigh. He had been gored while trying to rope a wild bull. "He cannot ride, you understand," Luis said. "He is sick with fever."

"How far is your camp?"

"I have been riding since before daylight."

Get help, Kern thought. Hugo Hendryx' radio might bring a doctor from Mexicali tomorrow. Or the next day. "Can an airplane land there?"

Luis shook his head and shaped a narrow "V" with his hands. "It is deep in the barranca."

"Is there a field anywhere near, some level place, if we could get a helicopter?"

"Only a bird can alight from the sky in the barrancas. It is all up and down."

"I'm sorry," Kern said. "I wouldn't know how to treat him. I'm not a doctor."

"You are the doctor's helper."

I'm just the flunky, Kern wanted to say. I can dab a cut or hand out pills, but I'd probably pass out cold at the sight of blood. "I'm sorry," he said again. "I can't leave the clinic that long."

Luis regarded him with sad dark eyes and lifted one shoulder in resignation.

"When did it happen?" Kern asked.

"Five days ago." Luis turned to his horses and swung into the saddle.

Kern moistened his lips. Dear God, he thought. Five days in this heat! But I just can't do it. "Luis, if I give you some medicine, bandages—"

"I can treat a calf for screwworms or the bloat. But this is my brother." Luis shook the reins and turned his horse into the road.

118

Kern stared at his retreating back with a sick, empty feeling. He could think of a dozen reasons why not to go. Reasons? Or excuses? But somebody had to go, somebody had to try. And he was the only somebody around. "Luis," he called, "that wound can't wait?"

Luis looked back. "No, *Señor,* it cannot wait."

"Then we can't either. Come on!"

He led Luis inside to the office and got the thick medical handbook down from the shelf. Four years ago he'd passed his Boy Scout First Aid tests. In gym last fall he'd taken a six weeks' hygiene course—social hi-jinks. That was it, his total medical experience. "Luis," he said, "tell me about your brother's wound, exactly as you remember it."

Luis did, and Kern broke out in sweat as he listened to the details. Opening the handbook to the index, he looked up various subjects: INFECTION, ANTIBIOTICS, SHOCK, STERILIZATION, FEVER. While he read and jotted down a list, Luis watched him with stoic patience. "We may not need all this," he said, "but—"

Luis nodded. "Understood."

Out of a bewildering array, first from the surgical chest and then the medicine cabinet, Kern made his selections: scalpels, lancets, wickedly sharp instruments whose names he didn't know; sulfa, powdered penicillin, distilled water, hypo, and syringe, compresses, gauze, and tape. The pile on the desk grew. Do-it-yourself kit, he thought grimly, Doc Dawson's sure-cure home remedy. "Is the trail rough?" he said. "Can your horses—"

Again Luis anticipated him. "I have been packing horses since I was a *niño.* Be assured nothing will break."

"Then I guess we're ready."

"Eat first," Luis said. "There is time for that."

Kern gulped a few mouthfuls at Mama Rosa's table and left a message for Bull. By the time he returned to the clinic Luis had packed the equipment into two leather bags stuffed with dry grass and secured one to the skirt of each saddle. He adjusted Kern's stirrups and motioned him to mount. As they rode out single file Kern glanced back and saw Ramón standing by the clinic door, sketchbook clutched under one arm.

Ramón raised an arm and Kern waved back. He'd forgotten the nightly art lesson. He hoped he hadn't forgotten anything more important.

Luis led him up the ravine past the village well and into the hills. They climbed steadily up a deep worn trail, raising a fog of pumice dust that coated riders and horses in gray. Following Luis' example, he tied his handkerchief over his mouth and nose, but nothing relieved the eye-watering irritation. Each hill looked exactly like the last, only higher, rising in endless swells toward the distant mountains.

As twilight faded into dusk the plants seemed to take on weird deformed shapes: pot-bellied elephant trees, giant ribbed cardóns, spiny ocotillo. A pitahaya became a many-armed Hindu god, an agave a warrior on the skyline. The air felt drier, and not a bird cry or coyote howl broke the stillness. There was only the plop of horse hoofs and squeak of saddle leather.

Just before dark Luis stopped and they rinsed out their mouths from his canteen. "It is your turn to take the lead," he told Kern. "I will eat dust for a while."

"How much farther?" Kern asked.

120

"Many kilometers. We have only started."

A quarter moon shed its radiance over the landscape and Kern found it easy to pick out the trail, which led up and up, always up. Once he looked back, but a shimmering pall of dust hid the Gulf far below. Luis had dropped behind several yards, a faceless black shape in a high crowned hat who looked as if he were part of his horse. Twice more they traded positions, and at the fourth stop Luis dismounted and said, "We rest here."

"You don't have to stop for me," Kern said. "I'm okay."

"The rest is for the horses."

When Kern slid down to the ground his knees buckled and he almost fell. His thigh bones felt like rubber. He waited for Luis to laugh or make some crack, but the ranchero was busy gathering twigs. He built a tiny fire, brewed coffee in a can, and produced a bag of jerky, while Kern slumped against a boulder and eased his aching legs.

After they had eaten Luis handed him a pair of chaps. Kern tied them on without question. Luis, he was beginning to discover, had a reason for everything. Somehow he remounted and minutes later, where the trail dipped into a canyon, he learned the answer. *"Chirinola,"* Luis said.

Kern had heard of "creeping devil," the cactus of evil repute that spread close to the ground and sometimes covered solid acres with its vicious barbed stems. Here it had grown stirrup high, hemming in the path to a narrow gap, a sea of cactus that stretched from wall to wall. "Do not guide your horse," Luis said. "Give him his head. He sees better at night than you."

Kern shook his reins loose and kept his eyes fixed on

Luis' back as they plodded ahead. If I look down, he thought, I'll blow it; I'll see that stuff and choke up. Several times the thick stalks scratched against his chaps, and once his horse came to a snorting trembling halt. Luis glanced back, clucked soothingly, and the horse moved forward again. Then they were clear of the worst of the cactus and Luis stopped. He lit a stub of candle, pulled out a pair of pliers, and examined the animals' legs for thorns.

Kern unclenched his hands from the saddle horn and said, "Doesn't that creeping devil ever close the trail?"

"Every year," Luis said. "Every year my brother and I chop it out."

"You go in there, on foot, with knives?"

"With machetes. On foot, yes. How else?"

Beyond the canyon the country grew rockier and more rugged. Buttes and jagged spires loomed up like the battlements of a vast medieval city. The moon had sunk behind the mountains, but the horses kept up their surefooted pace in the starlight, their iron shoes now and then striking off tiny sparks. To Kern it seemed they had been riding through an endless night, that his body was paralyzed below his waist. I won't be able to stand up for a week, he thought.

But gradually the sky lightened and shadows melted under the first flush of dawn. They labored up a steep rough pitch and Luis reined to a stop. "Barranca," he said. "Not far now."

Kern stared down at a narrow chasm, hundreds of feet deep, into which the trail suddenly disappeared. It was as if some berserk giant had slashed the earth with a cleaver. "We ride down—there?"

"*Sí*. You have only two legs. The horse has four."

Kern nodded weakly, grabbed the saddle horn again, and closed his eyes.

The sun was peeping over the rims before they reached the bottom of the barranca and level ground once more. Without a halt for rest Luis rode along the dry rocky stream bed and the horses pricked up their ears. In a moment Kern saw why. They rounded a bend and came upon a cluster of palm trees and a small pool of water, the first since they had left the village well.

A shelter built of hand-adzed palm trunks stood at the foot of the cliff. Luis exchanged a solemn look with Kern, stepped down, and walked to the entrance. Kern sat welded to his saddle listening to the rustle of wind through the dry roof thatch and the drone of bees. The camp had an abandoned lifeless look, as though the last occupant had departed long ago.

Had they traveled all this distance and arrived too late?

CHAPTER 12

Luis ducked inside and Kern heard him speak in a
low voice. The silence grew until it seemed to press against
his eardrums. Then Luis reappeared and said, "You must
rest before you see him. You are tired."

Kern was almost afraid to ask. "How is he?"

"No better."

As Kern's feet touched the ground his legs collapsed
and he fell. Luis helped him over to a palm tree and
brought him a dipper of water from the pool. "Do not be
ashamed of your legs," Luis said. "You rode well. Now
sleep a bit."

"When did you sleep last, Luis?"

Luis made a gesture that said it was of no impor-
tance.

"Make a fire," Kern said. "We'll need hot water. Lots
of it. I'll be ready then."

Luis nodded and went to the horses. Kern forced himself to step away from the supporting tree trunk. His legs

trembled but did not buckle under him. He tried a second step and a third, then began to pace slowly back and forth. After several minutes he could walk almost normally. When he returned to the shack Luis had a tub of water simmering over the outdoor fire pit. *"Bueno,"* he said and drew a deep breath. As he stepped through the doorway he felt as he had the moment they'd ridden over the rim of the barranca, as if he were dropping into space. But this time he had no saddle horn to cling to.

The brother lay motionless on his back in a bunk against the rock. When Kern bent over him José's eyes flickered open and he muttered a few unintelligible words. Despite the gauntness of his face and the pallor of his skin he looked much younger than Luis, Kern thought, young enough to be his son. Trying not to gag at the smell that hung thick and heavy in the hot still air, he said, "How do you feel?"

José twisted his mouth in a grimace.

Kern squeezed his shoulder and very gently folded back the blood-crusted cloth that covered his right thigh. As he peered down at the swollen flesh puckered around the wound, nausea seized him and his legs almost gave way again. Then he felt Luis' eyes on him. He straightened and stepped back to survey the room. The bunk would have to serve as operating table. There was a long shelf, a palm log split in half, that would hold the instruments. Next he examined the ceiling.

"I'll need more light," he said.

Luis climbed up and with his machete chopped a hole in the thatch, while Kern unpacked the saddle bags and spread out the items he had chosen at the clinic. The medical handbook he laid beside the bunk where it would be handy. Then he went out to the fire and thoroughly scrubbed his hands with soap and brush. "The horn didn't go deep," he told Luis, "but there's dirt in the *cornado.* That's the danger."

"What is required of me?"

"I'm going to give him a morphine Syrette. You may have to hold him. Then—" He said a little prayer under his breath and turned back to the shack.

"La Virgen te ayude," Luis said. "The Virgin help you. Both of you."

. . . It was past noon when they finally left José, freshly bandaged and sleeping quietly, and stepped outside. The fire under the tub had burned out, but tendrils of smoke still drifted into the cloudless blue sky. Kern felt lightheaded and mindless, as though his skull were hollow. Luis guided him into the shade of the palms. "I will sit with him while you rest," Luis said.

"Call me in an hour." Kern slurred the words. "We'll trade off."

When he woke up the canyon was blue with shadow and an evening star glimmered over the rims. Guiltily he jumped up, splashed cold water on his face, and hurried into the hut, where he found José asleep and Luis dozing on a bench. He lit the lamp, then checked the bandage and took José's temperature. The thermometer read 102.7. By dark it had risen to 103.5.

For the next thirty-six hours he and Luis alternated at the bunkside, while José fought his silent battle. They spoke hardly at all. There was little they could do beyond changing the dressing and sponging off José's hot flushed face. Luis cooked up a pot of frijoles, but neither had any appetite. They sat like zombies in the heat or snatched a few minutes of sleep and waited.

On the third morning the fever broke. Bathed in sweat, José tossed and turned and cried out for water. By midday they were spoon feeding him broth, weak as a baby but propped up in bed. "You see, *'manito,*" Luis told his brother, "soon you will be in the saddle again."

"What happened to the bull?" Kern wanted to know.

"He ran away." José managed a feeble smile. "Next time I'll rope the beast and dehorn him."

"Such craziness," Luis said sternly. "You think you are a picador in the ring in Mexico City?" But he smiled also, the first time Kern had seen him do so.

José improved rapidly. Next morning he was able to sit up by himself. He could even joke about his wound and the "battle" scar it would leave. By tomorrow or the next day, he assured them, he would be ready to ride home. But Kern was firm. José, he said, must remain at camp until the wound closed and he regained his strength, to which Luis agreed.

"But you," he told Kern, "are needed in the village. Tomorrow you must return. I will stay here with José."

"Go back alone?" Kern said. "Me? Over that trail?"

"The horse knows the way," Luis said.

For the first time in days—he'd lost track of the number—Kern thought of the clinic, of the Flying Buzzards and Bull Kalinksi and his job in La Ribera. And of the smuggler, if there were a smuggler. He knew that he would be sorry to leave the barranca, to say good-by to Luis and José. He was going to miss them when he got back to La Ribera.

That night they sat up late around the fire and talked.

127

Luis, who usually had little to say, told of cattle drives, of wild bulls he had known, of remote ranches tucked away in mountain oases where no visitors came from one year to the next. It was a land of few trails and no roads, a land unknown to the outside world.

"Is the camino—Smugglers' Road—the only road?" Kern said.

"There is no other," Luis said.

Kern hesitated, recalling the night he had first seen Luis. "Do you know anything about Ricardo, the truck driver?"

"Only that he drove too fast. He often passed my house."

"Some people think he was a smuggler."

"Perhaps he was."

"What do you think, Luis?"

"I think one should not speak evil of the dead."

"Ricardo's not dead. He's in the hospital in Mexicali."

Luis shrugged, rose to his feet abruptly, and said good night. He had found the truck driver in the ravine, perhaps had saved his life by going for help, but obviously he did not wish to discuss the subject.

Early next morning Kern packed up his gear and made a final inspection of José's leg. José, suddenly shy, grinned and gripped his hand. Someday, he said, Kern must come back; he, José, would teach him to ride like a *vaquero*.

With a catch in his throat, Kern mounted his horse and followed Luis up the barranca. They had agreed that Luis should accompany him as far as the rims, but

128

once the cabin fell behind and they rounded the first bend, Luis reined to a stop and got off. "Sometimes four legs are two legs too many," he said. "From here we walk."

Kern stared at him in bewilderment.

"You are an artist," Luis said. "I will show you something."

Once again Kern sensed it was not a moment for asking questions. They tied the horses in the shade and bulled their way through dense thickets of brush on foot. The canyon wall looked solid, a sheer towering cliff, but when they neared the base Luis led him around a granite slab and through a crevice into a narrow slot of side canyon. From a dozen yards away the entrance was invisible.

As Kern peered up the rubble-choked floor, he wondered what could possibly interest an artist in this barren place. Rocks? But he could understand why they had left the horses behind. With growing curiosity he followed Luis, crawling up slick water-worn slides, scrambling from boulder to boulder. In a wetter climate this once must have been a stream, he decided. There were potholes, pockets of sand, tangles of ancient wood washed down from the mountain crest, but not a trace of moisture.

They climbed for more than an hour, until the canyon widened and a grove of stunted palms came in sight. Luis sat down on a log and rolled a cigarette. "Now we wait," he said.

"Wait for what?"

"The sun."

The floor of the canyon lay in shadow, but gradually the sun's rays began to creep down the western wall, a descending tide of light. Mystified, Kern sat beside Luis and watched the color patterns change from a drab gray to glowing pink and chocolate. Once a hummingbird zipped by and a quail sounded its musical note. High in the sky a lone hawk hovered. "Long ago the Old Ones had a camp here," Luis said. *"Indios."*

"How do you know?"

Luis pointed out a deep cylindrical hole in a nearby boulder. *"Mortero.* They ground their seeds in that."

"There was water then?"

"Yes, before the great drought." Long before the Jesuits came to Baja, Luis said, the Indians of the barranca had died out or moved away. Perhaps their enemies had killed them off. Nobody knew for certain. Some people believed they had been a race of giants seven feet tall. "You have sharp eyes," Luis said. "See what else you can find."

Glancing at the ground, Kern saw it was littered with chips of black obsidian. In quick succession he turned up several fragments of pottery, a carved sea shell, two fire sticks of soft wood with tiny charcoal craters. An arrowhead, a scraper, half a dozen needles made of cactus spines. But one object—a cluster of stringy fibers attached to a bone handle—puzzled him. "It looks like a brush."

Luis nodded. "The light is right now. Come."

He rose and continued a short distance along the canyon floor, then halted and raised his eyes. As Kern looked up at the opposite cliff his breath caught. The rock wall, protected by an overhanging ledge, was covered with brilliant red and black painted figures, larger than life size— men, antlered deer, horned sheep. The human figures stood with upraised arms; many of the animals were pin-

130

cushioned with arrows, but all were done with surprising skill and sense of proportion. He thought of an Assyrian hunting frieze in a museum.

"They're beautiful, Luis! It—it's like an art gallery!"

"José discovered it one day hunting a stray cow."

Kern stared in wonder. Other Indian pictographs he had seen seemed crude and childlike by comparison, mere daubings on a rock. Unbelievable, he thought, to find such paintings here, here in a Baja barranca no one had ever heard of! How many months or years had it taken untold artists to cover that huge space? Where had they got the pigments? And how had they painted at all? Hanging in ropes from the cliff face?

"I think," Luis said, "they prayed to their gods for game, for food. That is the meaning of the arrows. But the springs dried up and the animals went away. So the Indians went away, too."

"And never came back?"

"And never came back. This was a sacred place." After a long silence Luis went on. "In my lifetime only two men have seen these paintings. José and myself. And now you."

Suddenly Kern remembered something Bull had told him once: These people don't have much money, but they have pride. And then he understood why Luis had brought him here.

"But you will come back. Many times, I hope." Luis touched his arm. "And now you must go. You have a long ride."

Long after nightfall he rode down off the last hill into La Ribera and felt the welcome dampness of salt air

131

on his skin. The clinic was dark, but a pair of village dogs set up a furious yapping at his approach and Bull stepped out from the house next door, followed by Mama Rosa. Kern got down wearily, grateful that his legs didn't betray him. Bull took the horse's reins and, much to his embarrassment, Mama Rosa hugged him hard and patted his cheek.

"Where you been?" Bull demanded. "You had us worried, boy."

"Didn't the *señora* give you my message?" Kern asked.

"Sure she did. But you've been gone a week. A whole week! I was going after you if you didn't show by tomorrow." Bull sounded more indignant than concerned. "What happened?"

Briefly Kern explained about José and his wound.

Bull's eyes widened. "You cut that kid's leg open? And doctored him? You did that?"

"I had to. That's what the handbook said."

"Handbook! Holy—" Bull stared at him and shook his head. "You go eat now. I'll unload the horse."

In her kitchen Mama Rosa fussed over him, piling more food on his plate and refilling his cup, all the while clucking like a mother hen. "El Toro, he worried so about you," she said. "All the time he worried."

I'll bet, Kern thought. Old Bull figured I'd lit out for good. That's what really bugged him. He said, "No fishing tonight?"

"No fishing," Mama Rosa said. "Every night he stayed home, expecting you to return, waiting for you. 'The boy

132

is lost,' he would say to me. 'The boy is hurt.' 'The boy has fallen off a cliff.' He blamed himself, you see."

"And what did you say, *Señora?*"

"I told him you are a man, not a child." Mama Rosa dimpled. "I know what you think. He stomps and snorts, that Bull, but underneath he has much heart."

Kern said, "Yeah, it's good to be home," and helped himself to a third piece of cake. About Bull Kalinski's heart he had his own opinions. Then he tottered off to bed and slept for fourteen solid hours.

CHAPTER   13

Late that afternoon Bull made his customary exit from the clinic with fishing rod and tackle box. Then he turned back and called to Kern through the doorway. "Almost forgot, there's a book for you."

"Book?" Kern said blankly. "What book?"

"Bob Garth left it when he flew down last weekend. On the desk."

Kern waited until he disappeared down the road and stepped into the office. The book was a fat volume from the San Diego Public Library dealing with pre-Columbian art in Mexico. Clipped to the first page inside the cover was the sketch Kern had drawn of the Whistling Monkey. Across the bottom Garth had written: "Your monkey led me a merry chase, but I finally ran him to earth, or his first cousin. See page 198."

So The Whip had remembered after all, Kern thought as he hastily turned the pages. Not only that, he'd gone to a lot of trouble. There were several photographs of bowls and jugs on page 198, including one with the familiar monkey handle. Kern bent closer to read the caption underneath and a current of excitement shot through him. He stared at the words, trying to absorb their significance, then bolted out the door and down the road to the waterfront.

Tony Vela, busy mending nets on the beach, greeted Kern with a grin. He and his grandfather, Tony said, had made a good albacore catch down the coast. And what was new with Kern?

"Remember that jug we found, Tony? It's even older than we figured."

"You're still stoked on that monkey, huh? Okay, how old?"

"You won't believe me. Come see yourself."

Tony shrugged and laid down his twine and they walked back to the clinic together. Kern showed him the photograph in the book and read the caption aloud: "Whistling vessel from the Monte Alban II period, *circa* 200 B.C. National Museum, Mexico City."

Tony whistled softly. "Over two thousand years old! That could be worth some coin."

"They don't put junk in a national museum. But where did our friend Ricardo get it?"

"Good question. What's this Monte Alban II jazz?"

Monte Alban, Kern read on the following page, was a mountain peak in the Mexican state of Oaxaca. A tribe of Indians called the Zapotecs, or Cloud People, built a city on the peak and founded a civilization that flourished for fifteen hundred years. They were the first Americans to domesticate plants, the first to practice writing and to live in cities. During their second period they produced wonderful works of art, including jade, life-sized pottery figures, bowls, and elaborate urns.

Around the year 900 A.D., Kern read, for some unknown reason the Indians moved away, the temples fell into ruin, and Monte Alban became a ghost city. Like the Indians of the barranca, the Cloud People had left behind their art and a mystery no man could solve.

"You sure this is the same jug?" Tony said.

"I don't think so. The markings are smaller." Kern got a magnifying glass from the drawer and studied the photograph. "We better check it out, though."

He led the way back to the storeroom and Tony helped him move the bags of cement. Long before they reached the bottom layer he knew the Whistling Monkey was gone. Someone had found his hiding place and stolen the jug.

The boys made a halfhearted search of the other rooms and gave up. Dejectedly Kern closed the book. *Nobody would ever think of looking behind those cement bags.* Words of wisdom from Kern Dawson, the dope!

"See if we can narrow it down," Tony said.

"How? Everybody in La Ribera knew about it. I was gone, Bull was gone. The place was wide open. Anybody could walk in and help himself."

"There's one place nobody walks in," Tony said. "Bull's room. How come he was gone?"

Kern told him about the trip Bull had taken in the jeep the week before.

"Business trip? Maybe that's where your monkey went. In one of those packages."

136

Bull had delivered another package, Kern remembered, the night of the truck accident. To the driver? To somebody in the village?

"How long was he gone?" Tony asked.

"Three days, he said. Maybe more."

"You can cover a lot of territory in three days. Maybe he had to take over after Ricardo got hurt."

"I still can't see a guy like Bull peddling old jugs."

"Why not? If there's money in it, much dinero? Let's look at that lock of his."

They walked around back and Tony knelt down to examine the padlock on the door to Bull's room. Kern watched uneasily while Tony fished a piece of wire from his pocket, sharpened it on a file from the tool kit, and inserted it in the keyhole. After several attempts the lock clicked open. "Where'd you learn that trick?" Kern said.

"Man, picking locks was kid stuff where I grew up. Every guy on my street had a record."

"You too?"

"I was in and out of Juvie like a yo-yo. Ancient history." Tony grinned and opened the door. "After you."

Kern peered in, still reluctant to enter, then stepped through the doorway. Bull's room was predictably neat, as G.I. as a barracks. There was the bunk, made up with square hospital corners; an olive-drab footlocker; a military field desk and folding canvas chair; a rack with two pairs of shoes polished to a high gloss; a suit and a jacket and a Marine Corps uniform hanging from an aluminum rod. Four decks of multicolored ribbons on the blouse caught his eye, only one of which he could identify —the Purple Heart.

137

The rifle he found on a shelf above the bunk, a World War II M-1, along with a metal ammo box full of cartridges in clips. A second box contained fishing gear—reels, lures, hooks—and a new baseball mitt. The footlocker held only clothes, folded in orderly piles. The desk obviously was too small for an object the size of the jug, but Tony opened the single drawer and poked inside. Presently he lifted out a looseleaf notebook, flipped it open, and said, "Hey, see this."

Across the top of the first page Bull had written in ink, "Paid to Gonzales." And under that a list of dates and amounts:

May 4	*$50*
June 25	*$75*
July 18	*$43*
Sept 9	*$86*

Over a period of fifteen months somebody, presumably Bull, had paid to somebody named Gonzales a total of $734. The last date was the preceding week.

"You know this Gonzales?" Kern asked.

"I know twenty Gonzaleses," Tony said. "It's like 'Smith' in the States. Could be anybody."

They puzzled over the meaning of the entries without reaching any conclusion, then finished searching the room. Of the Whistling Monkey they found not a trace. As he backed out the door Kern glanced at the uniform again, at the red sergeant's chevrons and the hash marks on the sleeves. He felt more than uncomfortable now; he felt ashamed.

Tony snapped the lock shut and said, "We learned

two things, anyway: Bull owns a rifle and he's making payoffs every month."

"Maybe he's buying his boat on the installment plan," Kern said.

"I'd like to catch the hombre that took a potshot at us, that's for sure."

"When can you get *Bobo* again, Tony? For Lizard Island."

"I'll let you know," Tony said. "But this'll be a daylight deal. No more night prowls for me. Not on Lizard."

After Tony had gone back to his nets Kern settled in his room with paper and pencil. Trying to organize his thoughts, he wrote down under the heading FACTS:

1. *Whistling Monkey, genuine, probably museum piece, value unknown.*
2. *Stolen from storeroom by X.*
3. *Came from Ricardo's truck. Maybe.*
4. *Power boat cruising at night without lights. Where?*
5. *Rifle shots on island. Who? Why?*
6. *Bull K????.*

The longer he stared at the paper the more confused and discouraged he became. Nothing added up or fitted together. Now that the one real piece of evidence was gone he wondered if he ever would unravel the truth.

As it turned out he didn't see Tony again for some time. Early next morning the Velas went south in *Bobo* for another run of albacore. Lizard Island remained a heat-blurred mystery on the horizon, remote and inaccessible.

Day after day the routine went on at the clinic. Some days no patients came at all. But there was always the maintenance, the cleaning and sanitation, the chore of hauling water. And there was Bull, whose sharp roving eye missed no detail, no smudge of dirt or speck of dust.

Word of Kern's ride into the barranca and his treatment of José had spread in some mysterious way, as news always spread in La Ribera. Villagers who had ignored him in the past often nodded to him now, or smiled at him on the road. One sultry evening when Ramón arrived for his lesson the boy surprised him by saying, "Someone wishes to see you."

"Someone sick?" Kern asked.

"He asked me to bring you to his *casa*. Felix the wood-carver."

It was the first time Kern had been invited into a home in the village. "You sure he wants me, Ramón, not El Toro?"

" 'Bring the artist,' he said. Felix, too, is an artist."

Kern put away his drawing board and accompanied Ramón. Felix' house, a small adobe adorned with potted geraniums at the windows, stood some distance up the beach. Kern had noticed it before and wondered at the flowers in this waterless land. As they approached, two elderly women in black *rebozos* came out crossing themselves and hurried off.

"The women of the village tend his garden," Ramón explained. "He carves relics for the holy places. A truly holy man."

There was something almost saintly about Felix, Kern decided a minute later, after he had shaken hands

140

and accepted a cup of coffee. Felix was sitting on a mat, his withered legs covered by a blanket, beside a low work-table which held his knives and tools and tubes of paint. A muscular man above the waist, he had wispy white hair and a gentle smile that erased the lines of pain in his face.

To Kern he said, "I have heard much about you." And to Ramón, "I thank you, *chico,* for sharing your friend with me."

Kern found he was at a loss for words, but Felix quickly put him at ease. "An old man seldom has young visitors," he said. "Tonight I am blessed with not one, but two."

The room smelled of glue and fresh wood shavings, and while Kern listened to the musical voice he glanced around at the shelves crowded with Felix' work: Madonnas, Christus figures, crucifixes, rosaries, saints, and devotional plaques and miniature shrines, all carved and decorated with exquisite delicacy. A Nativity scene, complete with lifelike animals, filled one entire corner. But as the evening wore on he began to suspect that Felix had summoned him here for a purpose that had nothing to do with art. Ever so adroitly he was being drawn out and sized up.

Presently the wood-carver sent Ramón home, observing that it was time for small boys to be in bed. When they were alone Felix sat for a while in silence, his eyes closed, as if he were at prayer. Then he smiled and said, "You have opened a door for our young friend with your drawing lessons."

Kern blushed and said that it had been his pleasure.

"You must wonder if I am an old fool talking in riddles," Felix went on. "I have lived here all my life, before

there was a village. I am older even than Serafina, the potter."

"That's hard to believe, *Señor*."

"Nevertheless true. I am not a priest. We have no priest
here. But because I am unable to go out in the world, the
world of La Ribera comes to me. Many tell me their troubles. And so I know there is trouble in our village."

Kern sat very still and waited.

"You know of the truck driver, Ricardo. He was not
an evil man, only weak and poor and easily tempted."
The wood carver paused. "But perhaps you do not know
that he is dead."

"Oh no, he's in the hospital. A radio message—"

"Some days ago I asked a friend who also drives a
truck to visit him at the hospital. The doctor informed him
Ricardo had been released. That same night"—Felix
sighed—"a car ran down Ricardo in the streets of Mexicali and escaped."

Kern felt his scalp prickle. What had Luis said about
Ricardo that night in the barranca? *One should not speak
evil of the dead.* "An accident?"

Felix turned up both calloused palms. "God alone
knows."

Or was it murder? Kern thought. Had Ricardo been
killed to silence him, because he knew too much? For that
matter how much did Felix know, as keeper of the village
secrets? "Do you believe he was a smuggler?"

"That is not for me to judge."

Felix lapsed into another, longer silence, his eyes
fixed on a medallion of the Virgin above the door. Like
Luis, evidently, he had said all he was going to say about
Ricardo. But Kern still waited, hoping for more.

When the old man did speak again he changed the subject. "I would like to ask a favor," he said.

"Yes, *Señor.*"

"I need a certain wood for a figure I am carving. *Palo fiero.* Ironwood. It is hard as rock. But all the ironwood trees near La Ribera have been cut down and burned long ago."

"Where can I get some?" Kern asked.

"There is a beach north of here where driftwood collects. Often one can find pieces of *palo* among other debris."

Kern nodded. It sounded like the beach where he'd cut firewood for Mama Rosa.

"I suggest you go some evening soon, perhaps tomorrow. The evening will be cooler. Take Ramón with you. He knows the way and what I need—only a small amount. Is it possible for you to perform this service?"

"I think so."

"I will be forever in your debt." The benign dark eyes regarded Kern searchingly. "I think you may find much of interest to observe there."

Like what, Kern wanted to ask, but didn't. Felix would give him some evasive answer or no answer at all. He was beginning to learn a little about these people. They told you only what they wanted you to know; the truth, especially if it might be unpleasant, they let you discover for yourself.

"Also," Felix said, "go with care. After sundown that is a lonely coast."

"You mean there might be some more—trouble?"

"Not if you are cautious. Otherwise I would not send you."

Felix was not to be drawn out further, and shortly afterward he said good night. Walking back through the darkness to the clinic, Kern puzzled over the meaning of the old man's request. In a way, he felt flattered. But why ask me, a stranger, he wondered. Felix must have many friends he could trust to do a simple favor. Unless collecting ironwood was only an excuse, a pretext to get him to a certain place at a certain hour—a lonely beach tomorrow night. It sounded as though Felix, in his roundabout fashion, had been trying to do *him* a favor, and warn him at the same time.

He'd go, of course. Nothing could keep him away. But I'm scared already, he admitted. Now that I know what happened to Ricardo.

CHAPTER 14

Some days at the clinic seemed longer than others, but the next day was the longest Kern had ever known. Each minute stretched out like a rubber band as he went about his chores. In his nervousness he broke a thermometer and dropped the sterilizer tray twice. Several times he caught Bull eying him thoughtfully. At the siesta hour he lay on his cot staring at the book on pre-Columbian art, as if that could give him the answer.

Eventually suppertime arrived, and afterward Bull departed for the beach. To Mama Rosa Kern tried to sound casual. "I notice your woodpile's getting low."

"Is enough for now," Mama Rosa said. "I'll tell El Toro when I need more."

Kern gave her a conspiratorial smile. "Let's surprise him. Maybe he'll give me Sunday off."

"You're a good boy," she said. "But no mischief tonight. He loves that jeep more than his mother."

When Ramón arrived with his sketchbook Kern told

him there would be no lesson because they were going to run an errand for Felix. It might take several hours. Would his parents worry? Certainly not, Ramón assured him. He was no baby. Eyes sparkling, he climbed in beside Kern and they rolled off through the village.

Kern drove north along the Gulf shore with a tingle of anticipation. Surely Felix had hinted at something more important than ironwood. Where the camino turned inland he stopped and deflated the tires, shifted into four-wheel drive, and followed the dim track toward the dunes. "What happened to Felix' legs?" he asked.

"He was born that way," Ramón said. "As I was born with a twisted foot. But there were no doctors then."

"Why do you want to be an artist, Ramón? Because of Felix?"

"Why do you?" the boy said. "Because of someone? Or just because?"

Kern laughed. "Good answer to a dumb question."

When the sand began to deepen he gunned the motor and the jeep climbed effortlessly over the dunes and hollows and coasted down to the smooth hard beach. It looked as desolate as ever, littered with wood of every description, some bleached as white as bone. There were no footprints or tire tracks, no sign that anyone had visited the place since Kern. "Does it have a name?" he said.

"Muerta," Ramón told him. "Dead Beach. Because all dead things float in here. Once even a dead whale." He rolled his eyes and pinched his nose. "Since then the *leñeros,* the wood gatherers, don't come so often."

"Happy hunting ground for scavengers."

Quickly Ramón found two dark heavy pieces of ironwood and Kern sawed up a load of stovewood. Then they wandered along the beach searching for bits of treasure. Ramón picked up an ancient pulley block, Kern a glass ball off a fishing net. There was one pine log with an ax blaze; it could have floated all the way down the Colorado from the mountains of Wyoming, he thought. But he saw nothing that had any bearing—not to him, at least—on smugglers.

When it was almost dark he drove the jeep several hundred yards back from shore and parked in a hollow. "Here's a blanket," he told Ramón. "Why don't you curl up in back and sleep."

"I'd rather stay with you," Ramón said.

They walked back and climbed to the crest of a dune that overlooked Dead Beach. Kern stretched out flat and the boy sank down beside him. The tide was coming in and they could hear the thud and crunch of wood against wood as logs rolled on the sand like alligators come to life. Two cormorants winged by as though bent on urgent business. Far across the water the spine of Lizard Island loomed up against the night sky.

"What are we watching for?" Ramón asked.

"I don't know. Maybe nothing."

"Is it part of the errand for Felix?"

"I'm not sure, but I think Felix wants us to be his eyes and his legs tonight."

Ramón accepted that and promptly fell asleep with his head cradled in his arms. And maybe I'm living in a dream world, Kern thought. If the old wood-carver knew something definite, why hadn't he said so?

The night sounds dwindled: an occasional bird cry, mournful and haunting, the swish of the sea on sand, the distant boom of surf up the coast. Kern missed his watch.

But maybe the waiting would be easier if he didn't know how much, or how little, time had passed. He envied Ramón breathing quietly beside him. Twice he caught himself nodding and slapped his cheeks to keep awake.

After the second time he noticed that a change had taken place in the sea itself. Each little wave curling inshore seemed edged with silver and broke on the beach into fiery greenish foam. He stared in fascination. The effect was beautiful, but ghostly, disturbing. Then he realized the tide must be phosphorescent.

The night was dark and moonless, and Kern had almost dozed off again when he heard the faint pulsation of an engine. Suddenly alert, he rubbed his eyes and peered out into the Gulf. At first the flat expanse seemed empty, then a black shape emerged from obscurity some distance offshore. Her exhaust burbling softly, the unlighted boat crept in closer like some blind creature sniffing out the land.

He prodded Ramón awake and clamped a warning hand around his wrist. "Take a look, Ramón," he whispered. "See if you recognize her from here."

The boy wriggled to the crest of the dune and elevated his head an inch or two. After a moment's scrutiny, he said, "There is only one big boat in La Ribera—*Señor* Hendryx' *Carefree*. But this one has no outrigger."

"Can't you take off the outrigger?"

"Wait until she turns. Then I can be sure."

The boat nosed ahead slowly as though feeling her way, peeling back a fiery bow wake. Then the engine died and she drifted silently until the anchor splashed and she swung broadside in the current a hundred yards or so off the beach, her high square lines in full silhouette.

"No," Ramón said. "*Carefree* is lower. They are not the same."

Smart boy, Kern thought. He has an artist's eye for detail.

For some while there was no sound or movement aboard the strange boat. Black and silent, she sat motionless in the silver-streaked water like some phantom ship, but now he could almost feel the impact of searching, probing eyes. Beside him Ramón began to tremble. "Nobody can see us, Ramón," he said. "Keep your head down."

"What if they come ashore?"

"We'll hide if they get too close."

Out on the boat a tiny light flicked on and off, followed by three longer flashes. Once, twice, three times the signal was repeated. Then blackness again. Kern rose on his elbows and risked a glance along the beach but saw no answering light, only dark empty dunes.

After another long wait, two figures appeared on deck and lowered some object over the stern. Kern's breathing quickened as he watched them climb in and cast off and head straight for Dead Beach. When they drew nearer he could make out the shape of a rubber raft, the kind scuba divers used. With each stroke of the paddle the blade dripped liquid fire.

Ramón tugged at his sleeve.

"Want to wait for me in the jeep, Ramón?"

"I'd rather stay with you. But—"

"They're not looking for us."

The two men waded ashore and pulled up the raft. It was impossible to see their faces. They could have been light skinned or brown, gringo or Mexican or Indian or

149

Chinese. They were figures, nothing more, twins of darkness from the sea. For several minutes they stood by the raft, turning heads this way and that as if ready to pounce in any direction. Once again Kern had an impression of hunters on the prowl. Whatever they'd come for, it wasn't driftwood.

The tide had started to turn after leaving its deposit of debris, its stench of kelp and dead fish and rotting pulp. One of the men snapped on a flashlight, shone it out toward the boat, and waved it once in a circle. Then they moved off together down the beach, walking slowly. Now and then they stopped and the light made a shifting bar on the sand.

Ramón wriggled closer and put his lips against Kern's ear, "They're looking for tracks."

So let 'em look, Kern thought. High tide washed out our footprints. Those creeps won't find a thing.

The man with the light let out a grunt and flashed his beam toward the base of a dune. They halted again and both knelt down. Heads together, they conferred. Suddenly Kern felt a lump crawl back in his stomach. Jeep tracks! From high-tide line his jeep tracks led all the way across the dunes. Fresh deep tracks they could follow like a freeway.

The first man winked his light at the boat. The second one sprang up and raced back to the raft. In a state of frozen shock Kern saw him grab a long black something that had to be a rifle. As he pivoted around, starlight glinted on the metal barrel.

Kern seized Ramón by the wrist and yanked him to his feet. Floundering down the reverse side of the dune, they ran for the jeep. Into the hollow, up the next steep slope they plowed through the soft resistant sand. At the crest he glanced back and saw a head appear over the dune behind. He dove from sight headfirst, hauling Ramón with him, and skied on his belly to the bottom.

"Barefoot!" Ramón panted. "Run faster!"

Kern kicked off his *huarches,* leaped up, and cut to his left down a gully. From below the dunes looked alike, identical pyramids of sand. He'd lost his bearings now, all sense of direction. Where was the jeep? This way? Over there? Like a squirrel in a maze he ran on with Ramón at his heels. Sobbing for breath, he floundered up to another summit. Behind and to his right the glow of a flashlight blossomed in the darkness and a yell went up. They'd cut his trail.

Then, across the sea of ridges, he caught a glimpse of a canvas top. "This way!"

With a gasp of pain Ramón stumbled against him. "My foot! You—go on!"

Kern groaned, dropped to all fours, and said, "Piggyback! Quick!"

He got Ramón on his back, gripped his thighs, and took off again, staggering from side to side like a drunk. Up, down, up, down. The dunes were mountains now, peaks that dragged at every step or crumbled treacherously to plunge him to his knees. Weaving, sliding, skidding, he climbed from ridge to ridge, bent almost double under Ramón's weight, which seemed to increase a pound per second. Something buzzed, and he jumped before he realized it was an insect. They fell in a tangle, and when he rolled over, there was the jeep in the next hollow—the beautiful, wonderful, marvelous jeep of Bull Kalinski's.

He dumped Ramón in and squeezed behind the

wheel. Frantically he dug in one pocket after another for the keys, then saw them dangling from the ignition. *Don't floor it, don't flood it.* The old Driver Training rule flashed through his mind. His hands were shaking so he could hardly find the starter button. He reached for the light switch and stopped. No lights. The guy with the rifle might be right on their tail.

The motor came to life with a roar that sounded like a jet to his ears. He babied the choke, gave himself a few precious heart-stopping seconds of warmup time, then gunned away. The tires chewed sand and took hold. Seconds later the jeep topped a dune as though shot off a carrier deck by catapult, wheels spinning in the air. "Hold on!" he shouted.

They landed with a spine-snapping jolt, and off toward the Gulf a flashlight beam stabbed across the night. Someone yelled. Kern poured on the gas and shot down behind another dune, spilling firewood at every bounce. He swerved inland to put a hill between them and the light, then eased up on the pedal. Several miles farther on they rolled to a stop at the *camino* junction, within sight of the low dark huddle that was La Ribera.

He slumped back against the seat and wiped his dripping face. "You okay?"

"Okay," Ramón said in a squeaky voice.

"The foot?"

"Better now. Sometimes, when I run too much, the foot —it hurts."

That Felix nearly got us shot tonight, Kern thought angrily. No, that's not fair. It was my own stupid fault. Felix did warn me. "Ramón," he said, "you'd make a great jockey at the Caliente track."

152

Ramón looked up with a shy smile. "Hello, horse."
They both broke into a spasm of wild semi-hysterical laughter.

Taking turns with the pump, they inflated the tires and drove on to Ramón's house in the village. Kern handed him the two hunks of ironwood. "Give these to Felix in the morning. Tell him what happened tonight, but nobody else."

Ramón nodded. "Why did those men chase us?"

"They didn't want anybody spying on them."

"Why not? What were they doing?"

"I think they came to meet somebody, only he wasn't there."

"Kern—" Ramón's voice had gone squeaky again. "Will they—do anything if they catch us?"

"How can they? It was pitch-dark. They didn't see our faces." But they saw the jeep, Kern thought. And there's only one jeep in La Ribera. It won't take a genius to figure out the driver. He ruffled Ramón's hair and said, "Get to bed now. Don't worry."

He parked behind the clinic and walked toward his room, soundless on his bare feet. Tonight he'd lost his sandals. Last week he'd lost his tennies. At that rate he'd be down to bedrock by the end of summer. If he lasted that long.

Bull's door was closed, the padlock in place. So El Toro hadn't come home yet. Had he been one of the two in the dunes? Or out in the boat! When did the man sleep? Kern shook the sand out of his clothes and dropped into bed, but sleep did not come to him at once. In his mind he kept seeing the glint of starlight on a rifle barrel.

CHAPTER 15

Kern was busy cleaning out the jeep the following evening when Luis rode up to the clinic. The ranchero dismounted and shook hands gravely. He had come to collect his other horse, he said, the one Kern had ridden, before he returned to the barranca.

"How's José?" Kern asked.

"Well," Luis said. "He does not ride a horse yet, but he sends his greetings."

"His leg? Is the wound healing?"

"Healing well." Luis permitted himself a rare smile. "You are a surgeon of surgeons. Perhaps medicine is your true calling."

Kern laughed. "Pity the next guy I have to operate on. That was luck and a prayer."

"Whatever, it had success." Luis glanced in the open doorway. "You are alone?"

Kern nodded. Bull had gone off again, without his fishing gear this time. Which was odd, come to think of it.

Odder still, Bull hadn't asked a single question about last night, as if he didn't care, or didn't know.

"Momento," Luis said. He turned to his horse and unfastened one of the leather pouches he used as a saddle bag. "Better that we go inside."

Puzzled, Kern led the way back to his room and closed the door. Luis handed him the pouch. "A present. From José and me."

Kern untied the drawstrings and pulled out an object carefully packed in dry grass. It was a bowl of reddish clay, about a foot high, with a handle in the shape of a head, a head of what looked like a three-horned demon with cruel eyes and bulging lips. It also looked old, centuries old, and familiar in certain details. "Luis! Where'd you get this?"

"I found it in the arroyo below my house," Luis said. "Where the truck crashed off the *camino*."

"You found it! When?"

"Two days after the accident." He had been rounding up his cows, Luis related, when he'd spied it in a clump of brush beside the wrecked truck. Everything else had been removed by then, so he'd carried the bowl home and left it there until today.

"Does anybody else know, Luis?"

"Only José. He thinks it's trash. 'Why don't you find something useful?' he says to me."

"José's wrong."

"He was also wrong about the bull that gored him." Luis smiled again. "My brother is young and has much to learn."

Kern grabbed the art book and opened it to the section on Monte Alban, leafing through the pages. On page

155

191 he located a photograph of a bowl not identical, but similar, to the one Luis had found. The caption read: "Effigy vessel, Monte Alban I period. Before 300 B.C. National Museum, Mexico City." It was older than even the Whistling Monkey!

"Luis, I—I thank you. But I can't keep this. It may be very valuable."

"I have only one brother. His life is valuable to me."

Kern swallowed. "How did you know the driver was dead?" He told him what he'd learned about Ricardo from the wood carver.

"I did not know. But men who live as Ricardo did usually do not live for long."

"Then he was a smuggler?"

Luis lifted one shoulder in a gesture that courteously, but firmly, told Kern he would answer no more questions. "I am a ranchero, not a policeman," he said. "The bowl is yours."

After he had ridden away Kern sat staring at the bowl. His! His to keep, to take home and put on the shelf above his desk in Oceanview. *A little something I picked up in Baja,* he would nonchalantly tell his family. *Only about twenty-three hundred years old. The Cloud People of Oaxaca. There's one like it in a museum in Mexico City.* He could see his sister's eyes bug out. Even his mom would be impressed.

And then he remembered that possibly a man had died because of this bowl. Suddenly the clinic seemed awfully still and cold.

He thought for a long while about possible hiding places. When it grew dark he stepped out, placed the ladder against the side of the building, and climbed to the roof. Removing the tank lid, he tied the bowl to a protruding rivet head with a length of cord, so that it dangled just above the water level. Then he replaced the lid, climbed down, and buried the ladder under a thin layer of dirt from the trash-pit hole.

Nobody—but nobody—was going near that tank except himself.

During the rest of the week he had to refill the tank only once, and he managed to do it when Bull was not around. When Bob Garth flew down for the weekend, he decided, he'd tell Garth the whole story. It was getting too complicated for him. Garth would know what to do. But Saturday morning came and went and no plane appeared. Gazing out at the empty airstrip, he said to Bull, "Looks like the boss won't make it."

Bull nodded. "Be quiet around here today and tomorrow. Why don't you take the weekend off?"

Kern stared. "You sick or something?"

"I'm sick of you. Take off. Get lost. Go somewhere."

Like where? Kern thought. Swim out to Lizard Island? Hike into the barranca twenty miles and back? Go scavenging at Dead Beach and get shot? "How did Garth happen to pick this place for a clinic?" he said. "Out of all Baja?"

"The way I heard it," Bull said, "Garth drove down here with a pal on a fishing trip a few years back. Got as far as La Ribera and busted his arm somehow. Had to ride back over that blankety-blank road for three days with a compound fracture to reach a doctor. So he decided to do something."

"How did you get here?"

"Me? I like to fish. Best fishing in the world right

here. And I get paid for it." Bull jerked a thumb at the door. "G'wan now. Shove off."

Kern gathered up his paints and easel and climbed to a low hill behind the well. If I spent twenty summers here, he thought, I'd never savvy that El Toro. But as he began to sketch the village spread out below against a dazzling backdrop of beach and sea, he shut the problem from his mind. It was almost dark when he returned, hungry and tired and sunburned, but with a glow of satisfaction. His painting might not win any prizes, but he thought his father would approve.

Early next morning he was awakened by a dribble of cold water on his bare chest. He sputtered and opened his eyes and saw Tony's grinning face. "Rise an' shine," Tony crowed. "Today's the day."

"Huh? What day?" Kern dried himself on the sheet. "When did you get back?"

"Last night. The old man said I could have the boat. So we're off to Lizard Island."

"Okay, but keep your voice down. You'll wake the Bull."

"He's not here," Tony said. "Unless he's Houdini. His door's padlocked."

Out all night? Kern wondered. Or had El Toro got up before sunrise? He dressed quickly, and as they hurried down to the bay front he told Tony about his experience at Dead Beach.

Tony's eyes widened. "The hombre with the rifle? Man, I wish I'd been there!"

"Man, be glad you weren't. I never was so scared."

Half a dozen fishermen were gathered around the turtle pens, inspecting two tortoises that had been captured the day before. Kern saluted them and helped Tony gas up *Bobo*. At this hour the air felt clean and fresh; across the water Lizard Island stood out as clear as an etching against the pearly morning sky. As they got under way Tony pointed to a boat drawn up on the beach. "Bull's skiff," he said. "He's not out fishing."

"He didn't take the jeep," Kern said. "So where is he?"

Tony had no answer to that, and they soon forgot the matter in the sheer pleasure of chugging across the flat calm sea. To the south the headland stretched out like a black gnarled finger pointing toward the invisible mainland of Mexico. Off its tip two small boats, part of the village fishing fleet, rode at anchor. Shortly Kern realized that Tony was bearing on a course that would intercept them, ninety degrees away from Lizard. "How come?" he said.

"Somebody could get curious," Tony said. "We don't want company."

As *Bobo* passed abeam he gave a hail and got a hail in return and continued in the same direction. After half an hour, when the shoreline had fallen far astern, he came about and headed northeast for the island. Theirs was the only boat in sight. "Foxy," Kern said. "You didn't learn that in Juvie Hall."

Tony laughed. "From my grandfather. He doesn't like competition following him. Let 'em find their own fish, that's his motto."

By the time they closed on Lizard the sun had transformed the surface of the Gulf into molten glass. Oily and opaque, it heaved in long green swells. Tony had heard of a landing on the far side, and he throttled down the engine. Escorted by swarms of gulls, they crept along under the cliffs. Even in daylight the place had a grim and hostile look.

Around the next point they came upon an indentation that could hardly be called a cove, but it did offer an anchorage of sorts. If they got caught in another blow they could haul out in a hurry. Tony cupped his hands and yelled, a sound which echoed off the cliffs and stirred up a cloud of birds. "Nobody here but us chickens," he said. "Let's go ashore."

Carrying canteens and lunches, they waded in through waist-deep water and climbed up through a crack to the top of the rims. From this vantage point they had a view of the island's eastern face. Lizard appeared to be about three miles long with a north-south backbone which terminated in the hornlike peak they had noticed earlier. An occasional spire of cardón stood out against the guano-splattered rock. Kern's hopes sank. Any footprints the rifleman might have left would be impossible to find in all this barren wind-swept jumble.

They climbed on to the central ridge, however, and began their search, working the side draws and gullies systematically. Faint threads of trails, apparently worn by animals in an earlier time when water had been plentiful, led everywhere. Even the big boulder where the boys had taken cover—where Kern had lost his flashlight—eluded them. Like the hills behind La Ribera, every rock on Lizard Island looked the same.

Their one discovery, high on the flank of the horn, was a tiny seep of brackish water. The few animal pellets and the ancient skeleton of some rodent in a nearby crack told them nothing. As Tony put it, this was the living end.

160

Even rattlesnakes couldn't make it here. Kern agreed; it was strictly for the birds.

In midafternoon they labored up the summit cone of the peak and were rewarded with a stunning panorama. In every direction the Gulf unrolled beneath them. Far below *Bobo* resembled a toy boat in a pond. The boys ate their *tortillas* and cold broiled yellowtail and discussed what to do next, whether to keep hunting in the few hours of daylight left, or quit and go home. "I hate to admit we're licked," Tony said.

"Me too. But we need an army to comb this place." Kern finished the last of the fish, walked to the dropoff, and tossed away the bones.

"Litterbug," Tony said.

"Tony, look! We stopped too soon!"

Tony stepped over beside him and peered down at a cove on the northeast tip of the island, a rock-free cove of deep-blue water with a crescent of white sand beach. A cove that could shelter half a dozen good sized boats. They hadn't been able to see it from the landward side before because of a double tier of cliffs. He whacked Kern on the back. "Sharp eye, man. Maybe this is it!"

It was a steep roundabout climb down into the cove. Breathless, they dropped onto the beach an hour later. The sand above the high-tide line was cluttered with fairly recent footprints. At least two men had made them, Kern decided, and a third party had been wearing *huaraches* soled with zigzag rubber tread from a tire casing.

The boys separated, searching toward opposite ends of the cove, and presently Tony called him back to inspect a ring of fire-blackened stones. It appeared to be a camp site that had been used more than once. There were a few charred twigs, two empty chili-pepper cans with the paper still intact, a mound of coffee grounds, and some scattered fishbones. "Who'd ever camp here?" Kern said.

"Hard to tell. Maybe some *vagabundos*. Even Seris."

"Seris?"

"Fish Indians. They used to live on Tiburon Island. Cannibals."

"Cannibals? Aw, come on!"

"So help me. My grandfather says in the old days they cooked up sailors who got shipwrecked there." Tony grinned. "That's why the government moved 'em to the mainland."

Kern gave him a skeptical look. Grandfather Vela seemed to be an authority on almost everything. Still, the story could be true. This Sea of Cortez had some history. Pirates. Smugglers. Buried treasure. Lost missions. Seven-foot Indians. And man-eaters, yet! "Three guys camped," he said, and stared up at the visible portion of Lizard Island's spinal ridge. "They could've shot at us from here."

"We didn't see their fire," Tony pointed out.

"They wouldn't be cooking at midnight. Not even cannibals." Kern scuffed the sand around the fire pit and kicked up an oblong of gray cardboard. It was a discarded match folder from which most of the cover had been ripped away, leaving a triangular stub with three printed letters: *dad*. "Who's dad?"

Tony examined the folder and shook his head. "Grandad? Dear Old Dad? Big Daddy? Doesn't ring a bell."

They searched for some while longer but found nothing more, and at last gave up. Leaden with weariness and disappointment, they climbed back to the anchorage, where they had to swim out to *Bobo* because the tide had risen. Even Tony's offer to troll for roosterfish on the way home failed to bolster Kern's spirits. He'd been so sure that Lizard held the key to the mystery. If so, probably they'd never crack it now.

Evening shadows lay over La Ribera when they pulled into the landing. Once again they drew sly smiles and expressions of sham sympathy from the pescadores as they stepped ashore empty-handed. *Ah, no catch today, Señores? A shame! Perhaps you used the wrong bait. Next time if you wish to hire a competent guide—*

"Drop dead," Tony muttered.

Early next morning, he told Kern, he was leaving for another long run down the Gulf that might take him away for several days. Sooner or later, he said, they would turn up the riffeman; they couldn't miss. But he said it without conviction.

As Kern plodded up the road alone he tried to project himself into the minds of the three campers on Lizard Island. Poor Mexican fishermen usually didn't buy store coffee; they ground their own beans. So they'd been rich fishermen. Or gringos. The kind that cruised in big power boats and owned high-powered rifles. Like the pair who'd tried to jump him at Dead Beach.

And *dad?* Who was *dad?* He studied the empty match booklet again. Maybe I'm asking the wrong question, he thought. Not who. But what. What is *dad?* In front of the clinic he came to an abrupt halt. For several seconds he stood by the door, his forehead creased in thought. "Bull" he called. "Bull."

But Bull hadn't returned. Kern got the keys from the office and hurried to the jeep.

CHAPTER 16

As he drove past the airstrip he nearly lost his nerve and turned back. This had ceased to be Dick Tracy stuff, a game of cops-'n'-robbers. Tony Vela was great, but at this point he wished he had an adult to carry the ball, a cool head like Bob Garth. A hunch and a scrap of cardboard wasn't much to go on.

Kern braked to a stop and reconsidered. He had to give Hendryx an answer about the job offer. He'd put it off too long already. If he dragged his feet much longer Hendryx might get suspicious. After a minute he drove on slowly.

Beyond the sprawl of low sandy hills he dropped down into the next bay and turned under the entrance arch of Hugo Hendryx' resort. The American's cruiser lay at her mooring off the beach. Eying her low trim lines, Kern decided Ramón had been right: *Carefree* wasn't the boat they'd seen at Dead Beach. A lean hawk-faced man who looked pure Indian stepped from behind the Land-Rover, which was parked alongside the main building. He carried a wrench and his hands were black with grease, as though he'd been working on machinery.

"Is *Señor* Hendryx here?" Kern said.

The man's glance shifted to the jeep and came back to rest on Kern. Then he moved his head all of a half inch in the direction of the front door.

The lounge was deserted, but the sound of voices carried from a room somewhere in back. Kern listened a moment and cleared his throat. Abruptly the voices stopped. After a silence, broken only by the throbbing of the gasoline generator outside, Hendryx appeared in the opening behind the bar. His eyes, curiously magnified by his thick lenses, fixed on Kern unblinkingly, and then he smiled in recognition. "Why, hullo there," he said. "How are you, Kern?"

"Fine," Kern said. "Mr. Hendryx, I—"

"Not another accident, I hope. The transmitter broke down. Need some new parts."

"No, sir. Not an accident. You see, I—"

"Well then, make yourself at home." The resort owner bustled out from behind the bar and shook hands. "How about a cold drink? Refrigerator still works, thank goodness."

"No thanks. I have to get back—"

"How's the clinic these days? Bull still cracking the whip?"

Kern had forgotten about the man's habit of interrupting every other sentence. He said quickly, "I came about that job."

"I'd about given up on you." Hendryx patted his paunch with both hands as if it were an old friend who needed reassurance. "How soon can you start?"

"That's the problem. I've been thinking things over and I hadn't better take it."

"Pay not high enough? Maybe I can raise the ante a little."

"No, sir, it's not the pay. I meant to tell you sooner but we've been busy and—"

"Maybe you heard some gossip about me, eh? What happened, Kern, I used to hire local people to run this place. A cook, a mechanic, so on. Frankly, they weren't much good. I had to fire the lot and hire some other people from Sonora. They resent that in the village." Hendryx paused. "Is that the reason? Be honest now."

"It's like this," Kern said, hoping his nervousness wouldn't betray him. Since Hendryx had come in he hadn't heard a sound from the back room, but he had an eerie feeling that someone was still there, listening to every word. "When Mr. Garth hired me I sort of promised to stick at the clinic all summer. I'd like to change but—"

"You would?" When Hendryx smiled he looked like a hungry shark. "None of my business, but I think you got in trouble back home. I think Bob Garth sent you to La Ribera to work it off. He's a born do-gooder. Am I right?"

Red-faced, Kern nodded.

"Why not do yourself some good? You told me you needed money for art school. Here's your chance."

"I appreciate that, Mr. Hendryx. But I'll be going back to Oceanview in a few weeks."

166

"You can always finish school. Plenty of opportunity for a bright young fellow in Mexico these days."

Acutely uneasy, Kern glanced around the room, at the mounted fish, at the walls. So okay, maybe the place needed sprucing up. But anybody could roll on a quickie coat of paint. What's that special about me? Why is he pressing so hard?

"Sixty dollars a week. How does that sound?"

"I—I guess I'd better do some more thinking." Kern swallowed. So far he'd been stalling, playing for time. Now he had to throw the curve, the big jug-handled one. "By the way," he said, fearful that his voice sounded shrill and artificial, "do you have an extra pack of matches? I ran out."

"Matches? Matches?" Hendryx blinked as though he'd never heard the word before. "Don't smoke myself." He fumbled in a recess behind the bar, fished out a cardboard packet, and tossed it underhand.

Kern caught the matches and stuffed them in his pocket. Edging toward the door, he said, "Thanks again, Mr. Hendryx. I—I'll be in touch."

"Let me know tomorrow. Time's a'wasting."

Outside in the fresh evening air Kern drew a deep breath. Maybe I should have my head examined, he thought, for ducking an easy job and sixty bucks a week. But that Hendryx is an oddball. The more he offers the less I like him.

As he approached the jeep he noticed the hawk-faced man with the wrench peering in the back. At the sound of Kern's footsteps on the path he straightened and stepped back. Not a muscle in the man's face twitched as they

167

stared at each other. This must be one of the "other people" Hendryx had hired in Sonora on the mainland, Kern supposed. He muttered good night and drove away. At the first curve he glanced in the rear-view mirror. Hawk Face was still standing beside the road, as motionless as one of Felix' carved wooden figures.

Once the hills were behind him he stopped and got out the match booklet Hendryx had given him. It was a standard commercial souvenir, the kind handed out by the thousands every day in California to advertise some store or motel or restaurant, but almost never in Baja. Across the folding cover, both front and back, were printed two words: "La Serenidad." The printing matched that on the stub he'd found at Lizard Island. *Dad* was La Serenidad. Serenity.

Kern struck a match and let it burn down. Somebody from Serenity had been at the camp site on Lizard recently. So what did that prove? Nothing yet. He needed more information, a lot more. Especially about the fancy resort with the fancy name where no guests ever seemed to come.

The next evening when Ramón arrived for his lesson Kern told him they were going to pay another visit to Felix. The boy came along without question and the old man greeted them courteously. He was seated on the floor by his worktable carving a small horse of some dark wood. To Kern the figure looked complete, perfect, but Felix continued to cut away minute shavings, using an assortment of tools that gleamed like surgical instruments in the lamplight.

He talked while he worked, about texture and grain, the problem of knots, about abrasives and finishes—a perfectionist to his fingertips. But he did not mention Dead Beach. As on the previous visit, Kern listened in silence, fascinated by the old man's skill. Presently Felix finished the carving to his satisfaction, rubbed it with steel wool, then sandpaper, and, finally, with some pungent oil until it glowed a rich red-brown.

He held the horse up to the light, squinted at it critically, and handed it to Kern. "Ironwood," he said. "For you."

"For me?"

"It is fitting. You rode a horse all night into the barranca."

"But I can't—"

"*Por favor.*" Felix raised a hand. "Say no more. When you go back to your country you will sometimes look at the little horse and think of your friends in La Ribera."

Kern exchanged a look with Ramón. The boy nodded. Kern rubbed his fingers across the satiny sheen of the figure and slipped it in his pocket. "Don Felix, may I ask a question?"

Staring at the floor, the old man seemed to have withdrawn inside himself, perhaps into his distant youth, before there had been a clinic or airstrip or *turistas* or even a village.

"How did you know about the boat at Dead Beach?"

For a minute he thought Felix hadn't heard. Then the wood carver smiled. "How did I know?" he said in a faint dreamy voice. "There are some who call me a gossip, a false confessor, and worse. But what I am told in confidence I keep in confidence."

"But you told me," Kern persisted.

"Because you can drive the jeep in which to haul wood, the only jeep in La Ribera."

"Will the boat come back?"

"I believe so, yes. But not there. They will be more cautious now."

"Where then?"

"There is only one other beach," Felix said and closed his eyes. His head nodded on his chest and he dozed.

Kern sighed. Stringing Felix' answers together was like braiding cobwebs. He motioned Ramón and they tiptoed out into the night. As they walked back to the boy's house under the stars, he said, "What beach did Felix mean? Those men aren't going to land their boat in front of the village."

"Don't you know?" Ramón sounded surprised.

Kern shook his head. Everybody in La Ribera seemed to know more than he did.

"Over there." Ramón pointed toward the headland. "The beach where *Señor* Hendryx lives."

It wasn't exactly information, Kern thought as he entered his room a few minutes later. But Felix had been right before. Maybe his hunch wasn't so kooky after all. He groped for the lamp and heard a noise outside. Stepping to the door, he called, "Bull? That you, Bull?"

There was only silence. Imagination, he decided. Then he heard a sound that made his skin crawl—a groan.

He snatched the flashlight from under his pillow and hurried out. As he rounded the corner of the clinic his beam picked out the figure of a man sprawled face down in the dirt. Bull! There was a nasty gash in the back of his head and a smear of dried blood. Kern knelt down and with an effort rolled him over. "Bull, what happened?"

The ex-Marine moaned and his eyelids flickered, then he slumped against Kern's knee. His face was pasty white and his skin felt clammy. Kern shone the light over him, looking for another wound, and felt his heart. But when he tried to lift him, Bull proved too heavy for his strength.

The house next door was dark, but he ran around to the side and tapped on Mama Rosa's window. Bedsprings squeaked and she came out at once, throwing a *rebozo* over her shoulders. "El Toro's been hurt," he said.

Mama Rosa gave a little wail and hurried along beside him. Dropping to her knees, she took Bull's head between her hands, and when she looked up Kern saw the glitter of tears in her eyes. "We must send for the doctor in Mexicali."

Kern clenched his fists until the nails bit into his palms. First Ricardo and now Bull. Only this was no accident. Somebody had slugged him from behind. "The radio's not working." When he saw the look on her face he added, "I don't think he's hurt that bad."

Mama Rosa bit her lip and nodded.

"Can you keep this secret, *Señora*—about Bull? From everybody? For a few days?"

"If you say so."

"Good. Now help me lift him."

Together they got Bull on his feet between them and half dragged, half carried him into the clinic and down the hall to the dispensary and laid him on the examination table. Kern lit a lamp and drew the curtains. *Pity the next guy I have to operate on.* Quote from that famous surgeon,

171

Sawbones Dawson. But this time, in his anger, he found himself surprisingly calm. With the aid of Mama Rosa and the medical handbook he clipped the hair from around Bull's wound, cleaned and disinfected it, and wrapped on a clumsy but airtight turban bandage. Through it all Bull lay unconscious, eyes closed and breathing heavily.

Even Mama Rosa produced a wan smile at his appearance. "My poor Toro, he looks like—an Arab."

"He's got a skull like the Sphinx," Kern said. "Lucky for him."

Once again they got Bull upright and piloted his limp two hundred pounds out the back door, across the sand, through Mama Rosa's kitchen, and finally into her bed. Kern mopped his forehead and handed her an envelope of sleeping pills. "If he wakes up, give him one of these. Keep him quiet. And if anybody asks—he's out fishing."

"How do you call it in English—fib?"

"We don't want the whole village in an uproar tomorrow. I'm sorry to put you out, *Señora*—"

Mama Rosa sniffed. "And who should nurse him? You?"

Hurrying back to the clinic, he went straight to the trash pit. The ladder lay undisturbed under the layer of dirt. So his bowl still was safe in the water tank. But the building had been thoroughly searched, room by room. Somebody had pried off Bull's padlock hasp and pawed through his desk and footlocker. Nor had his own room been neglected. On the woodwork he found a black smear of grease. But, so far as he could tell, nothing appeared to be missing.

The storeroom was a shambles. "They"—for some

172

reason Kern thought of Bull's attacker in the plural—had cut open several bags of cement and dumped out the contents. Obviously, so he reasoned, they knew their way around the clinic. They must have found the Whistling Monkey and come back to hunt for the second bowl. Since they hadn't found that, they might return a third time. Tonight?

Nervously he played his light back and forth across the night. Not much cover. But any man, or men, who could take El Toro by surprise must be very crafty indeed.

He searched the grounds around the building carefully and returned to the dispensary. Here, too, they had been at work, opening cabinets and pulling out drawers. The concrete floor, which he had freshly scrubbed that afternoon, was a tracery of dusty footprints—his own, Mama Rosa's, the squiggles left by Bull's dragging boots. In one corner he found the print of a *huarache*, a *huarache* soled with rubber tire tread in a distinctive crisscross pattern.

Only yesterday he had seen the same pattern, or one almost like it, in the cove at Lizard Island.

Kern blew out the lamp and stood in darkness listening to his heartbeats. Somebody, the shadowy "they," might be lurking anywhere outside, watching, waiting to make a final try. And now he had to admit that Bull could not be one of them.

Silently he slipped back to the house and into the kitchen. Through the doorway he saw Mama Rosa on her knees beside the bed, her head bowed in prayer over Bull's motionless bulk. As he started to back away, she pressed Bull's hand to her lips and laid her cheek against his forehead. Then, as if sensing Kern's presence, she gave a start and looked around.

He made a feeble croak intended as an apology.

A blush spread over Mama Rosa's face. She wiped her eyes and clutched the *rebozo* tighter about her. "You did not guess?"

"Guess what?"

"You ask if I can keep a secret," she said. "This is my secret, El Toro's and mine."

Kern stared at her dumfounded.

"We are married."

"Married!"

"In the eyes of God we are." She held her head high, eyes shining. "There is no priest in the village. One has not come for two years. We cannot wait forever. So we say the vows ourselves. *Union libre,* in Mexico. But until the priest comes we tell no one."

Such marriages were common, he had read, among people who lived far from a church. But Bull? And Mama Rosa? Right under his nose all this time! How blind could you be? "Well, gosh," he stammered. "That's wonderful."

Mama Rosa dimpled. "So now you share the secret with us."

He grinned foolishly. He'd been suspicious, all right, but for the wrong reasons. Night after night Bull had gone out fishing. Instead of meeting smugglers, he'd been coming back ashore after dark to Mama Rosa's house. That tough old, hell-for-leather, gung-ho Marine! Some secret! But it explained a lot of things.

"And the children. He loves them as if they were his.

He buys them clothes, sends them away to school. Oh, he is a good man, that El Toro."

Kern had forgotten the children, Mama Rosa's brood of five off in Santa Ynez. But now he remembered the brand-new baseball mitt on Bull's shelf. And the mysterious jeep trip with packages. A man could drive the round trip to Santa Ynez in three days, on "business."

". . . presents," Mama Rosa was saying. "He spoils them with presents. Dolls, baseballs, comic books. But he would be furious if he knew I'd told you."

"Sure. That's *our* secret, Mama Rosa." He patted her hand and checked Bull again. "Call me if you need any help."

Smiling to himself, he returned to the clinic. Now there was an idea that took some getting used to: Sergeant Bull Kalinski, husband and father, delivering toys to his adopted family like jolly old Saint Nick. Kern shook his head in wonder.

He got a blanket from his cot, uncovered the ladder, and climbed to the dark flat rooftop. Pulling up the ladder behind him, he spread the blanket and stretched out to sleep. He'd be safe up here tonight behind the water tank. But tomorrow, he suspected, was going to be the longest day yet.

CHAPTER 17

By sunrise Kern was up and off the roof, the ladder reburied. Smoke was already rising from Mama Rosa's chimney, and he hurried to the kitchen. Bull, she informed him, was conscious but groggy; he'd refused to take a pill.

Kern tiptoed into the bedroom, and Bull, flat on his back, opened one bleary eye. "How do you feel?"

"How do you think I feel?" Bull growled. "Lousy."

"Mama Rosa says you're a lousy patient. Won't follow orders."

"Who promoted you, Dawson?" Bull winced and gingerly touched his bandaged head. "Lordy, what hit me?"

"Guy with a wrench, I think," Kern said. "Didn't you see him?"

"I saw nothin'!" He had been checking inventory in the storeroom, Bull related, when he heard a noise. He'd stepped outside in the dark and rounded the corner of the building. Then— "Whammo! Next thing I know I come to here and it's daylight."

"Hendryx could be lying, but he claims his radio's dead. So we won't have a doctor before Saturday."

"Who needs a doctor?"

"You do. But if you stay in bed you may live till then."

Bull struggled to sit up, made a face, and sank back on the pillow. "Ooooow! I never felt this bad when I got kayoed in Korea." He balled the corner of his blanket in one huge fist. "When I catch that joker! What was he after?"

"Narcotics, I guess," Kern lied. This wasn't the time to explain his theory to El Toro: that the men at Dead Beach had seen the jeep and assumed the driver was the owner— one Bull Kalinski who ran the clinic of Baja Zopilotes. "Go back to sleep now and quit stewing."

"Don't think you can goof off while I'm laid up, Dawson. Scrub those floors."

"Yes, sir, boss. And use a toothbrush in the corners."

Bull's scowl gave way to a feeble grin. "Scram. Before my head busts wide open and spills what brains I got."

Kern spent most of the day at the clinic cleaning up the mess their visitors had left the night before. He made a second detailed search of every room and the grounds outside, but found no further clue to their identity. Not that he needed any; in his own mind he felt reasonably sure. But he was hoping for at least one solid bit of proof.

Fortunately no patients turned up for treatment.

177

Until five o'clock he had the day to himself. Then he heard the sound of a truck, and a man came to the door and asked for Bull in English. "Gone for the day," Kern told him. "Can I help you?"

"You can tell me where to unload this stuff."

"What stuff?"

"Look out front," the man said.

Apprehensively Kern went to the window. The vehicle parked outside was a typical truck of a typical Baja *maneadero,* rickety and loaded to capacity. The back was piled high with second-hand galvanized-iron pipe. "What's that for?"

The truck driver shrugged. "Bull still owes me sixteen bucks, but I guess his credit's good. Hasn't missed a payment yet."

Suddenly Kern recalled an item he and Tony had found in Bull's desk drawer: the notebook. In it Bull had listed a record of monthly payoffs to somebody named Gonzales. At the time it had seemed highly suspicious. But that was before last night. "Are you Gonzales?"

"That's me. Al Gonzales. I own the junk yard in Santa Ynez."

Kern felt a little dizzy. Once, a long time ago, Bull had told him: *You can't buy half a mile of pipe for peanuts.*

"Tell him I got that rotary pump he wants," Gonzales said. "I'll deliver it next week with the second load. Okay?"

"Okay," Kern said weakly. He knew now, or thought he knew, what the pipe and the pump were for. But he'd better stop jumping at conclusions. Where Bull was concerned his batting average had been .000. He helped Gonzales and his assistant driver unload their truck behind the clinic, and they went rattling off in a cloud of exhaust.

Mama Rosa had come to the door of her kitchen to watch. "What is this?" Kern said. "Another secret?"

She giggled. "A surprise. For everyone. El Toro is going to bring us water from the well. He hopes it will be ready by Christmas."

Kern stared at the mound of pipe in awe. A water system for La Ribera. No more washing clothes beside the tank, no more hauling water in ollas and goat carts and jerry cans. No more contamination, or maybe not as much. Water right in the village, fresh clean water! It sounded like a dream. A pipe dream, he thought, and grinned.

"You think he's loco in the head?" Mama Rosa said.

"I think he's *muy hombre.*"

"He says, 'This village has given much to me, so now I give a little back.' That's El Toro."

Kern poked his head in the bedroom, but Bull was sleeping quietly. He ate a few mouthfuls of supper and told Mama Rosa he had to do an errand at La Serenidad. *Let me know tomorrow,* Hendryx had said. Well, tomorrow was now. Tonight. With butterflies in his stomach he set out on foot in the early dusk, leaving the jeep behind.

He wished he had somebody with him, Tony or Luis, but they were gone. Ramón was too small. So he had to do it himself. He could still turn around and go back to the clinic and sleep on the roof again. Wait for Bob Garth to arrive on Saturday. Three more days. But suppose Garth didn't come? That meant another week, ten days. No, he couldn't wait that long.

He kept off the road, walking parallel to it some

distance away, ready to take cover if anyone drove past in either direction. By the time he'd crossed the low hills which separated La Ribera from the resort it was almost dark, and he felt more secure. The sand still held the warmth of the day and he crouched down behind an outcrop of rock overlooking Hendryx' place. To his left the headland reared up against the sky. Below, the waters of the bay lay flat as sheet metal in the rapidly fading light.

No light shone in any of the windows, nor aboard the cruiser moored offshore. The generator was silent, the Land-Rover absent from its usual parking place. La Serenidad, Kern thought, looked as serene and deserted as a graveyard. He took a roll of friction tape from his pocket and covered all but a narrow slit of his flashlight lens. After several minutes, when nobody had appeared, he crawled out from behind the rock and walked down to the beach.

The fact that he had a legitimate explanation for his presence did not reassure him as he moved silently up the entrance path on bare feet. If he did have to face Hendryx tonight he knew his manner would give him away. At the door he paused, then started violently when something zipped past his ear from under the eaves. A bat! When his heartbeats had subsided he pushed the door open and called, "Mr. Hendryx. It's me, Dawson."

He called again, twice, but there was no answer, only a rustling sound in the roof thatch as a mouse scurried away. Kern sucked in a breath, stepped inside, and snapped on his light. He went straight to the wall where the mounted fish hung and examined several specimens. They seemed okay, but there was something unreal about this place— something off key. He looked over the rest of the lounge,

180

the bar area, and the kitchen behind it, where he found a sink filled with dirty dishes.

There were two other rooms—a bedroom evidently used by Hendryx, and an office with a desk. The drawers contained odds and ends—old menus, a few more souvenir match booklets, a yellowed pamphlet boosting the charms of La Serenidad. Either Hendryx kept his private papers elsewhere or had destroyed them. I'm getting to be a pro at this, Kern thought, a full-time snoop.

Tonight he particularly missed his watch. He had no idea how much time he had spent going through the main building. Slipping out through a back door, he halted in the shadows and listened. One thing he'd learned on these night prowls: Never get caught by surprise. After waiting several minutes, he crossed to the nearest guest cabin.

All five proved disappointingly bare of interest. Twin beds with lumpy mattresses. Tables made of driftwood. Rusty clothes hangers. Layers of dust. Cobwebs. No guest had slept in any one of them for months. Which raised another question: If not off well-heeled gringo fishermen, how *did* Hendryx earn his living?

One building remained, a shack which housed the generator and radio equipment, but it, too, yielded nothing that could be called a clue. As a last resort Kern walked down the beach past the pile of gasoline drums and peered under the overturned rowboat. A crab scuttled across the sand. Zero.

So go home, Dawson, he thought. You flubbed again. Don't stretch your luck, man. He smiled as he thought of Tony Vela, wishing he were somewhere down the coast this minute dangling a line off *Bobo*'s stern.

The tide was phosphorescent, as it had been the night at Dead Beach, with ghostly green wavelets lapping at the shore. Crouched behind the rowboat, he gazed out at Hendryx' cruiser. *Carefree.* Serenity. The names that guy picked! She lay less than fifty yards out, an easy swim. After a moment's indecision he stripped down to his shorts, stuffed his shirt and pants under the rowboat, and waded into the water.

Paddling on his back so he could watch the resort, he swam to the cruiser with the flashlight elevated in one hand. He rested briefly on the anchor chain, then made a slow circuit of the hull. He could hear nothing, nothing at all. But surely he'd been at La Serenidad a long time now. Where was Hendryx? And Hawk Face? Had they gone for the night?

He got a grip on a stanchion and pulled himself up, dripping puddles on the deck. Under his feet *Carefree* seemed to shift with a slight but ominous roll, as though threatening to cast him off. Unfamiliar with boats of this size, he groped to a doorway and peered into a cabin. A companionway led farther aft and down a ladder into the sleeping quarters, a second cabin complete with bunks, galley, and a head.

He saw at once that *Carefree,* unlike the lounge ashore, did not suffer from sloppy neglect. No dirty dishes or unmade beds or cobwebs here. Everything gleamed. If Hendryx had an office anywhere, this was it.

Kern shone his slit of light over the bulkheads and stopped on a shelf above the stove. Three clay pots, everyday cooking pots like Serafina made, stood alongside several jars of poster paint. On one pot someone had tried to paint a series of red fishes, crude and amateurish shapes that looked more like droopy balloons. A sad pair of monkeys adorned the second pot. The designs on the third pot were unrecognizable, smeared and partially wiped off, as if the would-be artist had given up in disgust.

Kern's breathing quickened. There had to be some connection. Hendryx had asked him: *Can you paint fish?* Could that be the job, decorating pots for sixty dollars a week, pots that anybody could buy in the market place for a peso or two? Hardly. Serafina painted and glazed her own pots; probably she'd do well to make sixty dollars a year.

He stared out the porthole across the black band of water to the beach. Not a sound broke the stillness. In a burst of impatience he began to open drawers. In the end, Hendryx' hiding place proved ridiculously easy to find—a compartment under the second bunk.

Kern almost laughed as he reached in and touched the Whistling Monkey. It seemed like an old, old friend.

He glanced up at the jars of poster paint on the shelf and the picture clicked into focus, as though he'd punched a button. Suppose "they"—Hendryx—had a lot of valuable antique pottery to smuggle out of Mexico. So they cooked up a scheme to camouflage the stuff with fish or monkeys or whatever to make it look like gimcrack *turista* junk. The customs officers at the border weren't artists, or archaeologists. Once they had the pottery safe in California they wiped off the paint with solvent or maybe just a damp cloth. And presto! As easy as that.

And suppose the painter they decided on was a simple-minded high-school art student who'd be too scared to open his mouth once he got sucked in. He didn't have to be very good—just dumb. Kid named Dawson who happened to be handy.

All of a sudden he lost the urge to laugh.

And then he heard a sound that turned his knees to jelly—the throb of an engine. Kern stood quaking, powerless to move, his mouth dry as dust, heart thundering against his ribs. Then he snapped off the light and scrambled up the ladder. A power boat without lights was heading across the bay for La Serenidad, fast, plowing a fiery furrow in the phosphorescent water. The boat from Dead Beach. So Felix had been right again—dead right, you might say.

He crossed the deck to the land side and started to ease overboard when a pair of headlights came boring down the road into the resort. In a moment he could recognize the high boxy shape of the Land-Rover. It pulled to a stop on the beach. The headlights flashed off and on three times and went out. Two men stepped out—Hendryx and one other—almost as if "they" had timed it. This time, Kern thought, they had their signals straight. And there he was, caught between them, good old simple-minded Dawson, right in the middle.

Now tell Hendryx your story. *Mr. Hendryx, sir, I swam out to your boat to tell you I can't take that job. Sorry, sir. G'night, adios, and thanks a heap.* Pow!

He knelt behind a fighting chair in the stern and turned his attention back to the cruiser. She cut speed and coasted in, dropped anchor astern of *Carefree*. Kern made out two men on her deck, black faceless figures who uttered no sound as they swiftly lowered a rubber raft over

184

the side and climbed in. There was no wariness or uncertainty tonight. They'll paddle ashore and go inside, he told himself; when the coast's clear I'll take off.

Only they didn't. With a shock of disbelief he saw the raft glide not toward the beach but toward *Carefree*. Toward him!

He reached the rail in one long stride and lowered himself into the water, careful not to splash. Sucking in a lungful of air, he went down deep and scissored away from the boat, the only way he could go now, out, away from shore into the bay. When he surfaced he kicked over on his back in time to see the raft nose against the hull and the two men swing aboard. Kern opened his mouth for another gulp of air.

He was still too close, maybe twenty yards. But they hadn't seen him. It was going to be all right. God looks after fools and little children. Then he heard a sharp *"Aiyee!"* A slit of light snapped on. His light! The taped one he'd left on deck beside the fighting chair.

He flipped over and went down like a rock, real fear clutching at his innards. He was always leaving stuff behind—flashlights, shoes, clothes, canteens. The Case of the Careless Gringo. How many times had his mom lectured him? But this wasn't Mom. These guys used rifles. And now they'd find little puddles on the deck, wet footprints.

When he surfaced again he'd gained another twenty yards or so and his chest was heaving. Back on *Carefree* the men were running about and jabbering. From the beach Hendryx let out a roar. "Searchlight! Turn on the searchlight, you donkeys!"

Kern made his third dive. Shallow. What he needed now was distance, not depth. There'd be no cave to hide in this trip, no jeep waiting in the dunes. Just the great big empty Gulf. Next stop Sonora, sixty miles due east. Swim, you lunkhead, Swim! Up. Gulp. Down. Kick. Over and over, until his lungs felt on fire.

Exhausted, he floated on his back, gasping for breath. Aboard *Carefree* they had the searchlight on, a wicked beam that burned across the night like a giant blue-white laser. It swung in a lazy dazzling arc from north to south, converting the glassy surface into one endless prism. He lay motionless, watching as though hypnotized while it crept closer. Waiting until the last instant, he ducked under. The beam passed over him, slowed, and went on.

When he came up again he heard a new sound, the snarl of an outboard motor. Hendryx must have righted the rowboat on the beach and put her in the water. The light picked her up shortly, bearing out from shore, with a red-faced Hendryx seated in the stern and a hawk-faced man standing upright in the bow. Kern stared in horror. They shot through the beam, but not before he saw the pole Hawk Face held in his hand. Not a rifle. Harpoon. The kind the pescadores used for spearing turtles.

"Dawson!" Hendryx yelled. "I know you're here, Dawson!"

So they'd found his clothes. But they hadn't found him—yet. Grimly he struck out in a crawl for the headland. Three hundred yards. Maybe he could make it to the rocks. Then maybe— He stopped abruptly, sick as the realization hit him. Every splash he made, every stroke, every trudgeon kick, sent out little telltale neon ripples. Phosphorescent. In living color.

"Dawson! Can you hear me, you goofy kid? Sing out!"

Sure. Sing out. So your pal can prang me. I'm not a turtle, Mister. I don't even have a shell.

Very, very carefully he rolled over on his back. Sighting on the nearest rocks, he began a delicate flutter kick and paddled ever so gently with his hands. No splash. Slow but sure. After all, didn't the tortoise win the race?

Twice more he had to submerge when the searchlight swung over him. Once the outboard passed within a dozen yards, so close her wake rocked his body, but Hawk Face was looking the other way. And now the search grew disorganized. They cast about in wider and wider sweeps, shouting, cursing each other in sulphurous Spanish, until Hendryx' voice went hoarse. From *Carefree* they finally fired off a flare, a spectacular burst that turned night into blinding pyrotechnic day, but by then Kern had almost reached the headland.

He staggered into the shallows and flopped on a ledge just ahead of the still seeking light. When it had passed he crawled up into the rocks and dropped behind a boulder. He threw up then, all the quantity of salt water he'd swallowed, and hugged his shivering body. I made it! he told himself. I made it this far. Now if I can get out of these rocks into the hills behind La Serenidad—

A muscular arm gripped him from behind. A hand clamped over his mouth. Kern struggled wildly until a voice hissed in his ear, "Knock it off! 'S me, Bull."

187

Kern went limp until the arm released him, and turned around. In the starlight El Toro looked truly fearsome. Bare-chested, pajama bottoms tucked into his combat boots, bandage canted over his eyes like some crazy helmet, he held up his M-1 rifle as if it were a yardstick. "Bull! Your head!"

"Stuff my head. When you don't show at three a.m., I come looking!"

"How'd you know where to look?"

"Mama Rosa told me you went to Serenidad. Then I saw the searchlight." Bull made a gravelly sound in his throat. "Those goons hurt you?"

Kern felt his legs go limber. His voice didn't seem to work either, so he just shook his head. Like a movie, he thought unbelievingly. The late, late show. The Marines have landed.

"C'mon then. I got the jeep stashed behind that hill." Bull rubbed the rifle barrel affectionately. "I hate to pass up that stinker Hendryx. But he'll keep. He'll keep."

Kern peered around the boulder. The outboard was still darting along the perimeter of light like some frantic water bug, hunting, hunting—Hendryx would have a busy night, what was left of it.

"Keep low," Bull said. "Like me."

He seemed to melt into the rocks, a shadow barely seen. Following with difficulty in his bare feet, Kern felt a shiver play along his spine. El Toro *was* a pro at this, not a phony make-believe. I'd hate to have him hunting me.

Ten minutes steady climbing brought them to the jeep. Bull had left it here instead of barging in, he explained, because he'd heard the outboard and seen the

188

searchlight flare. In the Corps, he said, they hammered on you to scout the enemy. "Lookee first, then fight like hell. Old Marine proverb, boy."

"Enemy?" Kern said. "You knew about Hendryx all the time?"

"I knew he had to be a crook. Never did trust the bum." Bull tossed him a blanket and squeezed behind the wheel. "You can fill me in on the way."

"We going somewhere? Now?"

Bull started the motor and coasted down the slope. When they reached the road he flicked on the headlights and gunned across the airstrip and through the village. Kern peered back. "Fish Face won't follow us right off," Bull said. "Unless he walks. I snitched the rotor off his Rover."

"We're not going home—to the clinic?"

"Santa Ynez," Bull said. "Police post there. Radio. We'll get the law."

"Santa Ynez? But that's—"

"—up the road a piece. Smugglers' Road, that is."

"Smugglers' Road!" Kern glanced down at his bare legs. It figures, he thought. Smugglers' Road—in shorts and a dirty blanket. With a wild man in pajama bottoms. Maybe we can buy some pants in Santa Ynez.

Bull gave him a tigerish grin. *"Semper fi,* Dawson. *Semper fi."*

The police had come and gone, more police than La Ribera had ever seen. As Ramón remarked, there hadn't been such excitement in the village since a *chubasco* blew the roof off the turtle pens. Hendryx and his friends had

189

departed in their boats, but the mainland police had intercepted them in Guaymas. For the owner of La Serenidad, all Mexico hadn't been big enough.

"What'll happen to him now?" Kern said.

"Probably spend a few years in the *calabozo*," Bob Garth told him. "The government takes a dim view of foreigners looting national art treasures." Garth had flown south from Oceanview after the story broke in the newspapers, and now, ten days later, he was explaining the outcome of the case to Kern. "You have any idea how much some of those antiquities sell for in the states? To private collectors who aren't too scrupulous?"

Kern shook his head. He'd seen the last of the Whistling Monkey. And of the second bowl, which he'd turned over to the authorities.

"Up to thirty thousand dollars apiece," Garth said. "That adds up to big business."

"Where did Hendryx get his loot?"

"There was a ring. Well organized." Mexico was full of archaeological sites—"digs," Garth called them—all heavily guarded. But the ring found ways—bribery, theft, even murder—to break into the digs. The real problem was transportation, moving the treasures into the big money market of southern California.

"And I almost joined the gang," Kern said. "Brother!"

Garth laughed. "That was a slick scheme, camouflaging old pots. Would've worked, too."

Bit by bit, he said, the police had pieced together details of the operation. Gang members brought the contraband—bowls, sometimes statuary, masks, carved jade, vessels decorated with gold and silver—by boat to the

190

rendezvous point on Lizard Island and turned it over to Hendryx, who passed it on to Ricardo. Other members smuggled it across the border from Mexicali.

"But you were the fly in the ointment," Garth said. "When you and Tony stumbled across them at Lizard, they switched the meeting place to Dead Beach. Then, bingo! You again. So they had to use Serenidad. And that was fatal."

"No wonder they were frantic to get back those bowls that fell off the truck."

"Yes, poor Ricardo was the weak link in the chain. I doubt we'll ever know if he was murdered." Almost everyone in La Ribera, Garth went on, had suspected something wrong when fewer and fewer guests came to the resort, but perhaps only old Felix had guessed the truth: that Hendryx had turned to smuggling when his business went sour.

"You know," Kern said, "the village needs that resort. With the right guy it could bring in a lot of Yankee dollars."

Garth grinned. "Any candidates in mind?"

"Bull," Kern said promptly. "If he had some backing. He'd be great for fishermen."

"Bull, huh?" The teacher rubbed his chin and nodded. "Might be an idea. Incidentally, your mom—"

"Mom?" He felt a twinge of guilt. He'd written, sure, a letter faithfully each week. But Mom, his sister Beth, his dad, Oceanview—they all seemed a little hazy. Oh, he'd be happy to see them again when the summer ended, but the actual truth was—when you got right down to the bark —he hadn't missed them that much.

"She worries," Garth said. "All this news in the papers.

She thought maybe you'd want to fly home with me tomorrow."

Kern looked out over the village. In the twilight it looked a warm wheaten brown, as though the sun had toasted it. Funny I never saw it that way before, he thought; I'll have to paint it in this light. Home? Why, this—La Ribera, the Zopilotes—right here, this is home. "No, sir," he said. "I'd rather serve out my hitch."

Bull came sauntering over from Mama Rosa's house with a toothpick jutting from his mouth. He slapped the mountain of pipe piled behind the clinic. "Get your beauty sleep tonight, Dawson," he said. "Tomorrow we start digging."

"Tomorrow's Sunday," Kern protested.

"Gripe, gripe, gripe. Vacation's over, boy."

"Yes, sir. Right away, sir." Kern turned to Garth. "Mr. Garth, I'd like to ask one favor."

"Ask away."

"On your next trip could you arrange to bring a priest for the weekend?"

Garth frowned. "A priest?"

"Yes, sir. From a church. To hold services, perform ceremonies, things like that." Kern looked back at Bull and winked. El Toro had turned lobster red, from his neck to his hairline.

"I guess I could," Garth said. "But why?"

Kern grinned. "Wedding present for Sergeant Kalinski."

He hurried away then, down the road toward the beach. If he could find Tony they might get in a swim before dark.